Guardian for Hire

An Anna Gabriel Novel : Book 4

Georgia Wagner

Text Copyright © 2025 Georgia Wagner

Publisher: Greenfield Press Ltd

The right of Georgia Wagner to be identified as author of the Work has been asserted in accordance with the Copyright, Designs and Patents Act 1988

All rights reserved.

The book is copyright material and must not be copied, reproduced, transferred, distributed, leased, licensed or publicly performed or used in any way except as specifically permitted in writing by the publishers, as allowed under the terms and conditions under which it was purchased or as strictly permitted by applicable copyright law. Any unauthorised distribution or use of this text may be a direct infringement of the author's and publisher's rights and those responsible may be liable in law accordingly.

'Guardian for Hire' is a work of fiction. Names, characters, businesses, organisations, places, events, and incidents either are the product of the author's imagination or are used fictitiously. Any resemblance to actual persons, living or dead, and events or locations is entirely coincidental.

Contents

1. Chapter 1 — 1
2. Chapter 2 — 11
3. Chapter 3 — 21
4. Chapter 4 — 38
5. Chapter 5 — 50
6. Chapter 6 — 59
7. Chapter 7 — 63
8. Chapter 8 — 80
9. Chapter 9 — 86
10. Chapter 10 — 96
11. Chapter 11 — 106
12. Chapter 12 — 118
13. Chapter 13 — 128

14.	Chapter 14	141
15.	Chapter 15	157
16.	Chapter 16	167
17.	Chapter 17	179
18.	Chapter 18	192
19.	Chapter 19	204
20.	Chapter 20	213
21.	Chapter 21	228
22.	Chapter 22	237
23.	Chapter 23	250
24.	Chapter 24	262
25.	Chapter 25	273
26.	Chapter 26	284
27.	What's Next for Anna?	294
28.	Also by Georgia Wagner	296
29.	Also by Georgia Wagner	298
30.	Want to know more?	300
31.	About the Author	302

Chapter 1

Anna Gabriel's sneakers hit the weathered planks of the dock with measured thuds. Her ponytail swung in a steady rhythm as she maintained her jogging pace. To any observer, she appeared to be just another early morning runner enjoying the waterfront. But Anna's sharp green eyes constantly scanned her surroundings, cataloging every detail.

Russian docks on the Caspian Sea were never truly quiet, even at this early hour. Her ears picked up the distant rumble of cargo ships, the clanking of machinery, and the occasional shout of dock workers starting their shifts. She noted the positions of security cameras mounted on light poles and warehouses.

She'd been to Russia before, and the last time, she'd been told to never come back.

Certain... factions... would *love* to get their hands on "the Guardian Angel." Was it seventeen... no, sixteen confirmed kills on her last overwatch near the Caspian waters. And the Russians don't forgive lightly.

A burly man in a thick coat shuffled past, reeking of alcohol and cigarettes. Anna tensed, ready to react, but he stumbled on without a glance in her direction. She forced her breathing to remain steady, her face impassive.

She'd brought others with her this time. Three others. A company of four.

And it was on her shoulders to make sure they all lived.

Reaching Russia had been bad enough.

Anna's gaze darted to a rusted shipping container, barely visible in the dim light. She knew the threats lurking in the shadows of this port city. The FSB would have agents combing the docks, their cold eyes searching.

Worse than the FSB were the remnants of the Volkov Syndicate. Their tattoo-covered enforcers still prowled these streets, thirsting for revenge after Anna had dismantled their human trafficking ring three years ago. She could almost feel phantom fingers around her throat, a reminder of her last encounter with Dmitry Volkov himself.

A gull screeched overhead, nearly making her flinch. But she caught the reaction, keeping her body calm. She forced her breathing to slow, scanning the waterline for any sign of patrol boats. The Russian Coast Guard had stepped up their presence lately, their sleek vessels cutting through the waves with deadly purpose. One wrong move and she'd find herself staring down the barrel of an AK-74M.

A stray dog limped past, ribs visible beneath its mangy coat. Anna watched it warily, knowing that even strays could be trained as spotters by the local crime syndicates. Her fingers twitched, muscle memory from countless firefights urging her to draw her weapon.

But no one called her name. No one focused on her.

This was why she was here. Recon before any mission was imperative. She continued her jog, keeping her head down.

The salty air filled her lungs as she breathed evenly, her fit body easily handling the exertion. Her black hair, tied back tightly, revealed the distinctive streak of white—a remnant of stress from her military days that she'd given up trying to conceal. As she ran, Anna's mind moved just as quickly as her footsteps.

Tactical observation was a way of life to her.

Her gaze swept across the docked ships, identifying makes and models, estimating crew sizes based on their dimensions. A massive cargo vessel loomed to her right, its hull stretching several stories above the water line. Access point one. Two. She counted them as her eyes darted from one spot to another.

As ex-Navy, she would've been lying if she'd said there wasn't something soothing about being back near the water. Near ships.

Even Russian ships.

One particular ship was supposed to transport her to the location of an impossible mission in an inaccessible country.

But first things first.

She wanted to make sure the damn thing didn't have leaks. Of either variety.

The dock creaked under her tread as she passed a series of bollards, their thick ropes securing smaller vessels to the pier. She clocked the distance between each mooring point, filing away the information for potential use later. She glanced at a group of seagulls perched on a nearby piling, their sudden flight potentially signaling movement elsewhere on the docks.

As she rounded a corner, Anna's pace slowed imperceptibly. Her target came into view—a cargo ship.

The cargo ship towered before her, a behemoth of steel and industrial might. Its hull stretched nearly 300 meters, dwarfing the surrounding vessels.

Anna's trained eye immediately identified it as a Panamax container ship, likely of Russian origin. The faded Cyrillic lettering on its side read "Volga Spirit," though the paint was chipped and rusting in places.

She slowed her jog to a walk, her gaze methodically sweeping the vessel from stem to stern. The ship's bulbous bow protruded beneath the waterline, its hydrodynamic shape designed to reduce drag and increase fuel efficiency. Above, the forepeak rose sharply, leading to the forecastle deck where the anchor windlass and mooring equipment were housed.

As the observations cycled through her mind, she released a slow sort of smile.

In an odd way, it almost felt like a homecoming.

She released an exhale. "I've missed you," she murmured.

Her fingers moved to the tattoo on her forearm of a bone frog. It meant SEAL. As did the inked anchor on her wrist. Memories of three tours on three continents were hard to outpace, even at a six minute a mile clip.

And not all those memories were the sorts she *wanted* to recall.

Having gone to SEAL school, sniper school, and demolitions, Anna had been the ideal recruit for covert ops.

A term used to tidy up the real job: assassin for the government.

And now, she found herself still scanning the ship. A part of her wanted to retreat back to the US to her Class-C RV. Her home on wheels had a repurposed tank engine under the hood, and she missed the sense of familiarity.

Both her hands moved to her waist, double-checking where the Glock was concealed.

She could shoot just as well with *either* hand.

But tonight wasn't a night for shooting.

Just recon.

Casper, her old SEAL buddy, had promised it was all routine. He'd already set up the transport. All they needed was to show up bright and early tomorrow.

"I trust the guy," Casper had said. "Used to be Green Beret. If he brokered the trip, it'll be smooth sailing."

But as much as she relied on Casper's word... she wasn't so sure she trusted his contacts. Especially not those in Mother Russia.

What was the old adage? *Trust but verify.*

GUARDIAN FOR HIRE

This was the verification stage.

Anna approached the towering vessel, her footsteps careful on the worn planks of the dock. The ship's massive hull loomed above her, its steel plates pitted and scarred from countless ocean crossings. Rust streaked down the sides in jagged patterns, corroded by saltwater.

She paused at the gangway, eyes scanning the deck above. The ship seemed deserted, its deck bare save for stacked shipping containers and idle cranes. Wind whistled through the superstructure, carrying the scent of diesel fuel and brine.

A voice called out in the distance. "Ey, ty! Chto ty zdes' delayesh'?" a gruff voice shouted from behind her. Anna's muscles tensed.

She turned slowly, keeping her movements casual. A burly dock worker glared at her, his thick beard flecked with gray. His weathered hands gripped a clipboard.

"Izvinite," Anna replied smoothly, her Russian accent flawless. "Ya prosto zaglyadelas' na korabl'. On velikolepen." She gestured toward the ship with feigned admiration.

The worker's stern expression softened slightly. He grunted, nodding toward the vessel. "Da, ona krasavitsa. No zdes' opasno. Ukhodi."

Anna smiled apologetically and began jogging away from the restricted area. As she put distance between herself and the *Volga Spirit*, she caught snippets of conversation from a group of sailors huddled near a rusted shipping container.

"Blyad', etot reys budet dolgim," one complained, lighting a cigarette.

"Zатκnis', Ivan," another replied. "Khot' by my ne v Murmanske."

Their laughter faded as Anna rounded a corner, blending back into the early morning bustle of the port. The clang of metal on metal rang out as dock workers prepared for the day's labor. A tinny loudspeaker crackled to life, announcing arrival times in rapid-fire Russian.

The aroma of fresh blini wafted from a nearby food stall, mingling with the ever-present scent of diesel and salt air. A group of babushkas shuffled past, their colorful headscarves a stark contrast to the industrial gray of their surroundings. One clutched a string bag filled with potatoes and cabbage, likely destined for a pot of borscht.

In the distance, the deep bass note of a ship's horn reverberated across the water. Seagulls wheeled overhead, their raucous cries punctuating the steady thrum of machinery. A pair of stray cats darted between stacks of crates, their lean bodies a testament to the harsh life on the docks.

As she neared the edge of the port, the skyline of Astrakhan came into view. The golden domes of the city's cathedral glinted in the early morning sun, a reminder of Russia's complex history and the countless eyes that might be watching her every move.

She circled back around the opposite dock, approaching the same vessel from the west.

This time, she slackened her pace once more, spotting movement on the deck. She pulled a small, telescoping lens from the heel of her shoe. A gift from Waldo Strange III. She raised the lens, frowned, lowered it, adjusted the small device.

Anna raised the lens again, focusing intently on two men. Their movements betrayed their training, a language she could read fluently. The first man's stride was measured, each step precise and deliberate. He moved with an economy of motion. He constantly scanned his surroundings, head turning in increments—three seconds left, three seconds right, three seconds center. A rhythmic pattern.

The second man's posture caught her attention. His spine was ruler-straight, shoulders squared with military precision. Even in casual conversation, his hands never strayed far from his weapon. His fingers moved occasionally, almost imperceptibly, muscle memory from countless quick-draw drills.

As the two men conversed, Anna noted their positioning. They stood at angles to each other, never fully turning their backs on potential approach vectors. Their feet were planted shoulder-width apart, knees slightly bent—a combat-ready stance disguised as relaxed posture.

A gust of wind ruffled the first man's jacket, revealing a flash of kevlar beneath. Body armor on a civilian vessel. Anna's suspicions heightened.

The cargo ship was supposed to be a civilian vessel.

The men's eyes constantly swept their surroundings, even mid-conversation. They visually cleared sectors with practiced efficiency, their gazes lingering on shadowed corners and potential concealment spots.

One man reached up to adjust his cap, and Anna caught a glimpse of his wrist. A faded tattoo peeked out from beneath his sleeve—the distinctive insignia of a tier-one special operations unit. Her breath caught. These weren't just soldiers; they were elite operators.

Anna's eyes narrowed.

"What did you get us into, Casper?" she whispered.

Chapter 2

"Hey!" a voice suddenly echoed behind her.

She turned sharply.

Two men had emerged from a second, smaller vessel. The lights had been off, and the vessel secured. But judging by the sleek pistols in their hands, both these men had been stationed here as sentry.

Anna didn't move. Didn't blink. Didn't speak.

She waited, watched.

For now, all they knew was that a jogger had stumbled to the dock outside their big, scary ship.

"Hey, I'm talking to you!" snapped one of the men. He had an Eastern European accent but was speaking English. Because of the other soldiers with him, or because he knew who she was?

The approaching man's features were broad, his forehead flat. Polish? Czech?

She tried to place the accent.

Footsteps behind her suggested the two operators she'd spotted earlier were coming to investigate as well.

Two in front, two behind.

She didn't mind those odds. The element of surprise could handle at least a couple.

And the others?

Wait and see. Don't rush in. Old adages echoed through her mind like biblical commands, tethering her feet to the dock at shoulder width, hands ready for motion.

Twenty paces. Fifteen. The two men from the smaller ship moved rapidly, pistols aimed at her.

English because it was a western ship, she decided. They didn't know who she was. Otherwise, they wouldn't have gotten this close.

She took the time to gather intel. Information was vital and rapid observation was her specialty.

She scanned the approaching men, assessing.

The two men from the smaller vessel closed in, their pistols trained on her chest. Behind her, she sensed the operators from the cargo ship getting closer.

"Hands up!" barked the man with the Eastern European accent. His partner, a wiry man with a scar across his left cheek, flanked him.

Anna complied slowly, raising her hands. Her eyes never left the men, noting every detail. The leader's grip on his weapon was firm but slightly off-center—favoring his right side. Potential injury. The scarred man's gaze darted nervously between Anna and his surroundings. Less experienced, more likely to make a mistake.

"What are you doing here?" demanded the leader.

Anna forced a confused, innocent expression. She replied in nearly perfect Russian. One of the eight languages she spoke fluently. Six others were a work-in-progress. "I-I'm just out for a run. Is something wrong?"

The man's eyes narrowed suspiciously. He replied in Russian now, too. "This area is off-limits."

"I'm sorry, I didn't see any signs," Anna replied, her voice steady despite the adrenaline coursing through her veins.

She could hear the heavy breathing of the operators behind her. Four against one. She'd faced worse odds, but the situation was far from ideal.

Suddenly, a new voice cut through the silence. "What's going on here?"

A fifth figure had emerged at the end of the pier. This man could only be described as ostentatious. He boasted wealth the way a peacock flaunted its feathers. His suit was tailored, Italian by the cut. Gold glinted from his wrists and fingers. A heavy chain hung around his neck.

"I asked a question," the man said, his voice carrying the clipped tones of old money.

The two armed men from the smaller vessel hesitated, their weapons still trained on Anna.

"We found this woman snooping around, Mr. Blackwood," the leader reported, his accent thickening with nervousness.

Anna's mind raced. Blackwood. The name wasn't familiar, but the way the armed men deferred to him spoke volumes. A westerner, just like Casper had said. What was a western cargo ship doing in the Caspian Sea? Nothing good. But what type of nothing good mattered most.

Blackwood approached, his leather shoes clicking against the dock. He stopped a few paces away, appraising Anna with cold, calculating eyes.

"And who might you be?" he asked, his tone deceptively light.

Anna kept her hands raised, maintaining her facade of innocent confusion. She switched to English, but put on a heavy accent, as if she weren't a native speaker. "I'm sorry, I didn't mean to cause any trouble. I'm Anna. I was just out for, how you say... morning run."

Blackwood's eyes narrowed, searching her face. Anna met his gaze steadily, her heart pounding beneath her calm exterior.

"A morning run," Blackwood repeated, his voice dripping with skepticism. "Tell me, Anna, do you always bring a concealed weapon on your jogs?"

Anna's blood ran cold. Her hand reached involuntarily toward her hidden Glock.

"Don't," Blackwood warned softly. "My men are rather quick on the trigger."

The tension on the dock ratcheted up several notches.

Anna hesitated. Two options. Neither favorable. Keep playing the confused jogger? No. Not with this man. A peacock he might be, but his strut carried a hint of danger. And the crew he ran with? Ex special operators didn't come cheap—not even the retired type.

So she allowed her expression to go dark. One moment, she'd been wide-eyed, playing "panicked." The next, she went still and quiet.

Trained soldiers would recognize it as the calm before a cobra's strike.

Mr. Blackwood wasn't trained. Or he didn't care.

He sniffed at her. "Turkolu send you?" he asked. "I told you, the cargo ship is going to be cleared by tonight. Technically, I'm paid through the morning." He scowled.

Anna heard one of the operators clear his throat. The other kept his gun trained on her.

She shrugged. "Just seeing what the commotion was," she said simply.

There'd been no commotion. In fact, the dock was eerily quiet, the earlier morning bustle having died down, but now that she'd paused, she realized something else.

These five men were *nervous* too. Because of this Turkolu fellow?

She racked her brain. Bingo.

That was the name of Casper's contact—the man who'd organized the ship. Which meant *these* men were the customers *before* her. Their journey wasn't due to start until the morning. These men were disembarking.

She began backing away.

"Tell Turkolu he'll get his money!" snapped Blackwood. "And tell him to stop sniffing around. He'll get his cut when it's time." A sneer had crept into the wealthy man's voice. It suited him.

Anna stepped further backward, her eyes never leaving Blackwood's face. The tension in the air was palpable, like a taut wire ready to snap. She kept her hands visible, palms out, a gesture of non-aggression.

"I'll be on my way then," she said, her voice level and controlled.

Blackwood looked ready to refuse, but then he glanced at his expensive watch, muttered under his breath, and made a gesture as if to say *scram*!

The armed men lowered their weapons slightly, but their eyes remained fixed on Anna, their grip tense and ready.

She turned gradually, her sneakers pivoting on the weathered planks. The salty breeze tugged at her ponytail as she took another step away from the group. The cargo ship loomed in the water, its rusty hull a silent witness to the tense standoff.

As Anna moved to leave, a gust of wind carried fragments of conversation from the men behind her. Muttered words, barely audible over the lapping of waves against the pier.

"No more delay... women... shipment... good price..."

"Profitable..."

Anna froze, itching to reach for her concealed Glock. Cautiously, deliberately, she turned back to face the group.

"What sort of cargo do you have?" she asked, her voice low and foreboding.

Blackwood's eyes narrowed dangerously. "What business is it to you?"

Anna walked toward them, her green eyes hardening to chips of emerald. "What. Sort. Of. Cargo?" she repeated, each word clipped and precise.

The tension crackled like electricity before a storm.

Blackwood's face twisted into a grimace. "I don't believe that's any of your concern, my dear. Now, I suggest you run along before things get... unpleasant."

Anna looked between the men, assessing threats, calculating odds. The four armed men who had first confronted her, plus Blackwood. The cargo ship potentially housed more hostiles. Anna had faced worse.

Women. Profit.

Trafficking?

She thought of walking away. Of letting someone else's problem remain *someone else's problem.*

And then she thought of her sister, Beth.

What would Beth do?

Not much. Not damn much at all. Beth had been a stay-at-home mom until a few months ago, when her family had been ripped from her. It was still unclear if they were all dead, or if an arms dealer named the Albino had kidnapped them.

But Beth saw Anna as a larger-than-life figure. To Beth, Anna was a hero.

Could she just walk away?

Anna released a long breath. She massaged the bridge of her nose. "I really, really don't want to do this…"

"Scram!" snapped Blackwood. "Or we'll throw your pretty face in with the rest of those tramps. Actually, you know what... come here, doll. Let me get a look at you."

Anna faced the five men, rolled her shoulders once... And then she flashed a small, dead-eyed smile, peeling her lips back to show her teeth, like a shark before a feast. She dropped the fake Russian accent.

"I want to say sorry for what I'm about to do... But, to be honest... I'm not sorry at all."

And then the assassin-for-hire *moved fast.*

Chapter 3

"What do you mean we need a new *ship*?" Casper yelled into his phone, pacing in the small motel room Beth and Anna had rented.

Anna sat motionless in the worn armchair, her posture relaxed but alert. The ice pack on her knuckles had begun to melt, droplets of water trailing down her wrist and soaking into the frayed fabric of the chair. Her green eyes tracked Casper as he paced the length of the room, his agitation evident in every movement.

Russian motel rooms north of the Caspian Sea were surprisingly sparse. The faded wallpaper peeled at the corners, revealing patches of crumbling plaster beneath. A single bulb dangled from the ceiling, casting harsh shadows across the room's worn surfaces. The air smelled faintly of mildew and stale cigarette smoke.

Casper's nearly-shaved head gleamed under the harsh fluorescent lights, his weathered features twisted in frustration as he barked into his phone. The sunglasses he habitually wore, even indoors, were perched atop his head, revealing the deep lines etched around his eyes. His muscular frame, slightly softened by age and a desk job, was tense with barely contained anger.

The cheap carpet muffled his heavy footsteps as he made another circuit of the room. The room smelled of the cleaning spray Beth had tried to disguise the smoke with—citrus something.

Anna wasn't much of a homemaker. The only use for citrus she could think of was masking the acrid smell of cordite after a firefight.

Anna's gaze flickered to the window, where thin curtains did little to block out the neon glow of the motel sign. A car rumbled past outside, its headlights briefly illuminating the parking lot before fading into the night.

Casper ended the call with a vicious jab at his phone's screen. He stood still for a moment, chest heaving, before turning to face Anna. His eyes, normally hidden behind dark lenses, were sharp with anger and something else—fear, perhaps.

"We're screwed," he growled, his voice rough. "There was a shooting at the Astrakhan port last night. Five men dead, three more on the ship. And get this—they found a bunch of women locked up below decks. Human trafficking ring, by the looks of it."

Anna's expression remained impassive. "Huh."

"My local contacts think a hit squad tore through that place... Maybe Russian mob." He released a long breath. Casper ran a hand over his scalp, frustration evident in every line of his body. "The ship's in police custody now. It's not going anywhere, and neither are we. Dammit!" He slammed his fist against the wall, causing a framed print of a generic landscape to rattle precariously.

"Any leads on who was responsible?" Anna asked, her voice calm.

Casper shook his head. "Nothing concrete. Dock workers heard gunshots, called the cops. By the time they got there, it was all over. Professional job, from what I hear. No witnesses, no surveillance footage. Whoever did this knew what they were doing."

Anna nodded slowly, her face betraying nothing of her thoughts. She shifted in her chair, wincing slightly as the movement pulled at the bandage on her bicep. If Casper noticed, he gave no sign, too caught up in his own frustration to pay attention to Anna's discomfort.

"So what now?" Anna asked.

"Dropping eight bodies?" Casper snorted. "If we were in the USA, maybe it'd make the news. But here? It's like the wild west on the Caspian. Must've been a bloodbath."

Anna didn't correct him. In fact, it had been far more like a lethal, precise operation.

She hadn't wasted any movements.

Anna's mind flashed back to the events on the dock, replaying the scene in vivid detail.

She had moved with lightning speed, her body a blur. The first man barely had time to register her movement before her elbow connected with his solar plexus, driving the air from his lungs. As he doubled over, gasping, Anna's knee rose to meet his descending face with a sickening crunch.

Spinning on her heel, she faced the second attacker. His gun was halfway raised when Anna's hand clamped down on his wrist, twisting sharply. Bones snapped. The pistol clattered to the dock. Her other hand delivered a vicious palm strike to his nose, sending cartilage splintering into his brain.

The two operators behind her reacted quickly, but Anna was quicker.

Her hand found her concealed Glock. Two shots rang out in rapid succession. Two bodies hit the dock, red blossoming on their chests.

Blackwood stood frozen, his face a mask of shock and terror. Anna advanced on him, her movements fluid and predatory. He fumbled for a weapon, but Anna was on him in an instant. Her hand closed around his throat, lifting him off his feet with surprising strength.

"The women," she barked, her voice low and dangerous. "Where are they?"

Blackwood's eyes bulged, his feet kicking uselessly in the air. He managed to choke out a single word: "Below."

Anna nodded once, then slammed Blackwood's head against the side of the ship. His body went limp, sliding to the ground in a heap.

The entire confrontation had lasted less than ten seconds.

Back in the present, Anna's eyes refocused on Casper. She kept her expression neutral, betraying nothing of her involvement in the dock incident. "We'll need to find another way," she said simply, rising from her chair.

"There is *no* other way," Casper snapped. "You took the job. You told Byers you were in. He flew us to *Russia*. You think he'll fly us back just as quick? We can't back out now."

Beth stood nearby, watching the exchange. She moved back to the window in the room, peering out at the motel parking lot.

Anna noticed the tension in her sister's slim frame silhouetted against the dim light filtering through the cheap curtains. Beth's shoulders were hunched. Her fingers fidgeted with the hem of her oversized sweater, a nervous habit Anna recognized.

With a sigh, Anna rose from her chair, ignoring Casper's continued ranting about their predicament. She crossed the worn carpet, her footsteps silent, and came to stand beside her sister.

Beth's reflection in the grimy window glass revealed the toll of recent events. Dark circles shadowed her eyes, stark against her pale skin. Her honey-blonde hair, usually meticulously styled, hung limp and unwashed around her face. The soft curves of her features, so unlike Anna's sharp angles, were drawn with worry and fear.

Anna placed a hand on Beth's shoulder, feeling the slight tremor that ran through her sister's body at the touch. Beth leaned into the contact, seeking comfort she'd rarely allowed herself to accept from Anna in the past.

"We'll find them," Anna said quietly, her voice pitched low so Casper couldn't overhear. "Tony and Sarah are tough kids. They take after their mom that way."

Beth's eyes met Anna's in the window reflection. "I'm not tough," she whispered, her voice cracking. "Not like you."

Anna squeezed her sister's shoulder gently. "You're tougher than you think. Remember when you stood up to those mean girls in high school? Or when you worked two jobs to put yourself through nursing school?"

A ghost of a smile flickered across Beth's face, there and gone in an instant. "That was different," she murmured.

"No, it wasn't," Anna insisted.

Beth turned away from the window, facing Anna directly. Her eyes, the same shade of green as her sister's, were bright with unshed tears. "I'm scared," she admitted, her voice barely above a whisper.

Anna nodded, understanding the weight of that admission. "I know," she said softly. "But we're going to get through this."

Beth gnawed at the corner of her lip. "I'm going with you."

Anna sighed again. They'd already had this conversation, and Beth had won. They had argued for hours. Beth hadn't backed down. So Anna had conducted a tactical withdrawal. But there were strict parameters in play. It was against Anna's better judgement, but she was torn. The safest place for her sister, Anna had decided, was somewhere Anna could keep an eye on her.

Also, if the Albino really was the target, then one way or another, Beth would have answers about her missing family.

She'd allowed Beth on the plane.

But if Russia was dangerous then Turkmenistan was downright deadly.

Anna held up a finger, counting off the rules. Not just to remind Beth of her promise to follow Anna's lead, but also for Anna's own comfort. The protocol gave her a slow, lingering sense of reassurance.

"One," Anna said firmly, "you stay on the ship unless I tell you otherwise."

Beth nodded reluctantly.

"Two, you carry the satellite phone at all times and answer my check-ins immediately."

Another nod.

"Three, if anything goes sideways, you use the emergency beacon. No hesitation."

Beth's eyes hardened with determination. "I won't let you down."

Anna's expression softened slightly. "This isn't about letting me down. It's about keeping you safe."

Casper's voice cut through their quiet exchange. "Ladies, if you're done with the heart-to-heart, we have a serious problem to solve."

Anna turned, her posture shifting subtly. The softness vanished, replaced by the coiled readiness of a predator. "What's the play?"

Casper grunted. "I've got a lead on another ship. It's not ideal—smaller, slower, and the captain's reputation is... questionable. But it's our only option right now. Also a westerner. Only other one here, but big money."

"Big money?"

"Very big."

"And why are we going with a westerner?"

"Less likely they know someone local to sell our hide to. Besides, I'm not trying to fake a damn accent if we get pulled. Better to feign corrupt American. Easier play."

"When and where?" Anna asked, her mind already racing through potential scenarios.

"Tomorrow night. Different port, about fifty miles up the coast." Casper's eyes narrowed. "It'll be tight. Security's tighter after last night's mess."

Anna nodded, her face betraying nothing. "We'll make it work."

Beth looked between them, worry showing on her features. "Is it safe?"

Casper barked out a harsh laugh. "Safe went out the window a long time ago, sweetheart."

Anna shot him a warning glare before turning to her sister. "It's as safe as we can make it. Remember the rules we talked about."

Beth straightened, squaring her shoulders. "I remember."

Anna turned back to Casper. "You went a long way to vouch for Byers."

"I vouched for his money. And that check cleared."

"That check was only part," Anna returned. "Needed Waldo's participation. Where is he, by the way? His plane should've arrived yesterday."

"Was supposed to meet us at port. I'll let him know the location's moved."

"Fidgety fellow isn't going to like it."

"Yeah, well... the color green is brighter to him than yellow. He'll show. He needs the money."

"Just... remind me again how we know where the Albino is?" Beth blurted out. She winced quickly, sealing her lips.

Anna gestured to Casper as if to say *go on*.

Casper leaned against the wall, his muscular arms crossed over his chest. Any evidence of the pudge he'd put on during his retirement was now nowhere to be seen. In part, he'd been spending odd hours training Beth, but he also spent the early morning hours in the gym.

Anna wasn't sure what this resurgence of effort was attributable to, but she couldn't say she disliked it.

Casper had always been a good-looking man. And with his jawline returned, she was reminded of just *how* good-looking.

"We're not certain," Casper admitted, his voice low. "But if the Albino is who we think he is, we have a brief window where he'll be in Turkmenistan."

"Where is that?" Beth asked, her brow furrowed.

Anna moved to the rickety table in the corner of the room, unfolding a worn map with practiced ease. Her finger traced a path across the paper, coming to rest on a nondescript area bordered by Iran, Afghanistan, and Uzbekistan.

"Central Asia," Anna explained, her voice clipped and professional. "Former Soviet republic. Mostly desert and mountains."

Casper grimaced. "And one of the most closed-off countries in the world. Makes North Korea look like a tourist hotspot."

Beth's eyes widened. "How are we supposed to get in?"

"Very carefully," Anna replied, her gaze still fixed on the map. "It's not just the government we have to worry about. The place is crawling with drug traffickers, arms dealers, and religious extremists."

Casper agreed. "The Albino's got connections there. Deep ones. If he's holed up in Turkmenistan, it's because he feels safe."

"Which means we won't be," Beth whispered, her face pale.

Anna's jaw tightened. "The capital, Ashgabat, is a bizarre mix of opulence and oppression. Marble palaces and gold statues next to crumbling Soviet-era apartments. The secret police are everywhere."

"And in the countryside?" Beth asked hesitantly.

"Worse," Casper said bluntly. "Vast stretches of the Karakum Desert where you could disappear and never be found. Mountain ranges where tribal warlords still hold sway."

Anna pointed at an area on the map. "There's a reason they call part of the country 'the Gates of Hell.' It's a massive burning gas crater that's been on fire for decades."

Beth shuddered visibly. "It sounds like walking into a nightmare."

"It is," Anna confirmed, her voice understanding. "But it's our best shot at finding the Albino and getting answers about your family."

Casper pushed himself off the wall, his face grim. "We'll be operating without any official support. If something goes wrong, there's no extraction team, no cavalry coming to the rescue."

"And if we're caught?" Beth asked, her voice barely a whisper.

Anna and Casper exchanged a look heavy with unspoken meaning.

"Let's make sure that doesn't happen," Anna said firmly. "We have a long night ahead of us. We need to plan every detail if we're going to pull this off."

The room fell into a tense silence, broken only by the hum of the ancient air conditioning unit. Anna's eyes swept over Beth and Casper, taking in their expressions. She knew the weight of what they were about to attempt was settling on them.

"Alright," Anna said at last, her voice cutting through the heavy atmosphere. "Let's break this down step by step."

She pushed aside the cheap motel notepads and pens on the small table to make room. From her bag, she pulled out a well-worn notebook and another set of high-quality topographical maps.

"First, our insertion point," Anna began, her tone shifting to that of a seasoned military briefing. "The ship will dock at Türkmenbaşy, the main port on the Caspian Sea. It's heavily guarded, but that works in our favor—they're looking for threats coming in, not going out."

Casper nodded, moving closer to examine the maps. "I've got a contact there. Ex-Spetsnaz. He can get us through the initial checkpoints, but after that, we're on our own."

Anna's finger traced a route inland. "We'll need to move fast. Our intelligence suggests the Albino has a compound here, in the foothills of the Köpetdag Mountains."

Beth leaned in, her face pale but determined. "How far is that from the port?"

"About three hundred miles," Anna replied. "Normally a day's drive, but we'll need to avoid main roads and checkpoints. It could take us three days, maybe more."

Casper added, "And that's assuming we don't run into any... local hospitality."

Anna's jaw tightened. "Right. We'll need to be prepared for multiple scenarios. Tribal encounters, military patrols, maybe even rival criminal groups."

She reached into her bag again, pulling out a small, innocuous-looking device. "This is our ace in the hole. Courtesy of our friend Waldo Strange."

Casper raised an eyebrow. "What's that little gizmo do?"

"It's a multi-spectrum jammer," Anna explained. "It'll disrupt communications, disable vehicle electronics, and even mess with some weapon systems. But it's got a limited range and battery life."

Beth's eyes widened. "That sounds... incredibly illegal."

Anna's lips quirked in a humorless smile. "In Turkmenistan, breathing without permission is illegal. We're well past worrying about that."

She turned back to the maps, her expression hardening. "Once we reach the compound, we'll need to move fast. In and out, no more than an hour. The Albino's security will be top-notch, and we can't risk a prolonged engagement."

Casper nodded grimly. "And if he's not there?"

Anna's gaze met his, cold and determined. "Then we find someone who can take us to him... But all that is contingent on one thing."

He scratched his new jawline.

"Do we *have a boat*?" Anna asked. "Have you confirmed that lead will pan out?"

"We already had one," Casper replied, his eyes narrowed. "But someone ruined that for us." His gaze lingered on her a split second longer, suspicion in his attention.

She didn't bat an eye but did shift to hide the bandage on her arm.

Casper sighed when she didn't respond. "I'll get it done. But you're not going to be happy. Not one bit."

Chapter 4

"I'm not happy," Anna said simply, staring toward the boat.

The next morning's sunlight crested the horizon, staining the lapping blue waves in a golden haze. But the beauty of the ocean was lost on her. She crossed her arms over her chest, her eyes narrowing. "Casper... you're joking."

Her associate winced sheepishly at her side, rubbing at his jawline. "I told you, you wouldn't be."

If Anna had been the type for witty banter, she might've kept speaking. But she was more the strong, silent type, and right now, that silence was deafening, along with her disarming and frightening glare.

Beth sat in the car behind them, still gathering her duffel, along with some other items. The yacht loomed impossibly large, its sleek white hull gleaming in the early morning sun. It stretched at least 150 feet from bow to stern, its multiple decks rising like a floating skyscraper.

Polished teak decks caught the light, contrasting sharply with the gleaming stainless-steel railings. Floor-to-ceiling windows lined the upper levels, tinted to obscure the opulent interiors. A helipad was located on the top deck, large enough to accommodate a medium-sized chopper.

The vessel's name, *Golden Horizon*, was emblazoned on the hull in flowing gold script. Two jet skis hung from davits on the port side, while a speedboat bobbed gently in the water, tethered to the stern.

Anna's jaw clenched as she took in every ostentatious detail. The yacht screamed wealth and excess, drawing attention like a beacon. It was the antithesis of the discreet transport they needed.

"How are we supposed to slip under the radar with this?" she demanded, rounding on Casper. Her voice was low, but fury simmered beneath the surface.

Casper held up his hands defensively. "I know, I know. It's not ideal—"

"Not ideal?" Anna hissed. "It's a floating billboard. We might as well paint a target on our backs."

Beth had arrived now, laden down with an enormous bag into which it seemed she'd packed every item of *need* she could imagine. She stood a few paces behind, her eyes wide as she took in the massive vessel. "It's... certainly big," she offered weakly.

Anna ignored her sister's comment, her gaze boring into Casper. Again preferring the scald of silence.

Casper sighed, running a hand over his scalp. "Look, after the incident at the docks, our options were limited. This was the only vessel I could secure on short notice that could make the journey."

"And the owner?" Anna pressed.

"An... associate," Casper replied carefully. "He owes me a favor. Several, actually."

Anna's eyes narrowed further. "What kind of associate?"

Casper hesitated, then seemed to deflate slightly. "Arms dealer. Mid-level, nothing too heavy. But he's got connections in the region we're heading to."

"Dammit, Casper," Anna growled. "You know how risky that is. If he decides to sell us out—"

"He won't," Casper cut in firmly. "I've got enough dirt on him to ensure his cooperation. Plus, he stands to make a tidy profit if this goes well."

Anna turned back to the yacht, her mind racing through scenarios and contingencies. The vessel's size and luxury would certainly draw attention, but it might also provide cover. In a region where oligarchs and crime lords flaunted their wealth, they might blend in more easily.

Besides, time was ticking.

If the Albino was sitting still for now, there was no guarantee that would last. Paranoid types often kept moving.

Anna shook her head, muttering under her breath, but she shrugged beneath the weight of her own backpack—this one about half the size of Beth's duffel. For one, she'd forgone the M&M trail mix that Beth had described as *essential*. For another, she'd grown accustomed to packing light. Her spartan choices had once saved her life during a firefight in Kandahar.

Her mind flitted back, dragging a memory from deep in her subconscious.

Her team was scattered, comms down. She was alone, armed only with her rifle and what she could carry on her back. Every ounce mattered as she calculated her escape route.

The building shuddered as an RPG impacted nearby. Chunks of sun-baked clay rained down, coating her in fine powder. Through the haze, she spotted a narrow alley—her only chance at breaking out of the kill zone.

With practiced efficiency, Anna shed every nonessential item. The extra magazines went first, then the night vision goggles. Her fingers hesitated over the first aid kit before discarding that too. In the end, she was left with just her weapon, two magazines, and a single canteen.

She'd managed to make it out.

If Beth had been there, with her chocolate trail mix... Anna doubted her sister would've made it five steps.

She shook her head, muttering to herself and trying not to let her scowl crease her features.

Anna took a deep breath, pushing aside her reservations. "Fine. But we do this my way. No unnecessary risks, no drawing attention."

Casper nodded, relief evident on his face. "Agreed. I'll brief the crew—they're ex-military, discreet. They'll follow your lead."

Anna turned to Beth, her expression softening slightly. "Remember what we talked about. Stay below deck unless I say otherwise. Keep your sat phone on you at all times."

Beth nodded, her expression a mix of determination and fear. "I remember. I won't let you down."

Anna placed a hand on her sister's shoulder, giving it a gentle squeeze. She repeated the same sentiment from the night before. "This isn't about letting me down. It's about keeping you safe."

With that, Anna shouldered her pack and strode toward the gangway. Her eyes scanned every detail of the yacht, cataloging potential escape routes and defensive positions. Old habits died hard.

As they boarded, a tall, lean man in a crisp white uniform approached. His weathered face and sharp eyes spoke of years at sea. "Welcome aboard the *Golden Horizon*," he said, his voice carrying a hint of an Eastern European accent. "I'm Captain Yevgeny. We're ready to depart on your order. Just... once the second payment is cleared..." His eyes moved to Casper.

"Hang on," Casper snapped. "I've already paid. Second payment isn't until *after* the trip is completed."

Captain Yevgeny's eyes hardened, his posture stiffening. "I'm afraid there's been a change of terms. My employer insists on full payment upfront, given the... delicate nature of this voyage."

Anna's hand twitched toward her concealed weapon, her muscles tensing imperceptibly. Casper stepped forward, his voice low and dangerous. "That wasn't the deal."

The captain shrugged, his face impassive. "The deal has changed."

Anna placed her other hand on Casper's shoulder. "Pay him," she muttered. Then she turned her gaze back to the dock. "And where the hell is that asshat?"

By *asshat,* she meant the fourth and tardiest member of their undercover party.

Waldo Strange III always had a special talent for getting on Anna's nerves. She suspected his antics and wisecracks amused Casper, but if Waldo's technical know-how, hacking abilities, and access to illegal arms weren't so useful, she would have happily left him behind.

He was already running a quarter hour late. She scowled toward the dock's parking lot.

Her eyes narrowed as she searched for any sign of Waldo Strange. The man's chronic tardiness was more than just an annoyance—it was a liability. Every minute they delayed increased the risk of discovery.

Just as she was about to order Casper to make the call to leave without him, a battered van came screeching into the parking lot. It fishtailed slightly before coming to an abrupt stop, the suspension groaning in protest.

The driver's door flew open, and out tumbled Waldo Strange III, looking as disheveled and manic as ever. His wild hair stuck out at odd angles, and his rumpled Hawaiian shirt clashed garishly with his cargo pants. A pair of thick-rimmed glasses sat askew on his nose.

"Hold the boat!" he called out, his voice carrying across the dock. He stumbled slightly as he hefted an oversize duffel bag, nearly dropping it in his haste.

Anna's jaw clenched. "Cutting it close, Strange," she growled as he approached the gangway and joined the rest of them onboard.

Waldo flashed her a lopsided grin, seemingly oblivious to her irritation. "Ah, but I made it, didn't I? Had to make a few last-minute adjustments to our little toys."

He patted the duffel bag affectionately. "Trust me, you'll thank me later when these beauties save our collective behinds."

Anna glared at him, then turned to Captain Yevgeny. "We're all here. Let's move."

The captain nodded curtly, barking orders to his crew in rapid-fire Russian. The yacht's engines rumbled to life, a deep thrum that vibrated across the deck.

As they pulled away from the dock, Anna admired the horizon. The open sea stretched before them, a vast expanse of blue that held both promise and peril.

Beth appeared at her side, her demeanor a mix of excitement and apprehension. "This is really happening, isn't it?" she asked softly.

Anna nodded, her expression becoming grim. "Yes, it is. Remember, stay alert. Trust no one but me and Casper."

As if on cue, Waldo piped up from behind them. "Hey, what about me?"

Anna turned, fixing him with a withering stare. "You're useful, Strange. That's not the same as trustworthy."

Waldo clutched his chest in mock offense. "You wound me, Gabriel. And here I thought we were best friends."

"Enough," Anna snapped. "We need to go over the plan one more time. Everyone to the main cabin. Now."

As the group filed inside, Anna lingered on deck for a moment longer.

Her fingers brushed the grip of her concealed Glock, drawing comfort from its familiar presence. As the yacht cut through the waves, leaving the safety of the harbor behind, a sense of unease settled over her.

The others had already moved toward the main cabin, their shadows—caught by the sun to their back—were sent forward across the ground ahead of them.

Anna noticed her own solitary shadow stretching toward the retreating forms.

Briefly, her mind wandered. She didn't often allow it to do that. But she'd been feeling more and more tired over the last few months. A strange, bone-deep exhaustion.

The gentle lapping of waves against the hull filled the air, a rhythmic sound that should have been soothing. Instead, it only emphasized the sudden quiet, the absence of voices and movement. Anna's hand fell away from her concealed weapon, her fingers flexing restlessly at her side.

At the horizon the vast expanse of the ocean met the sky in a hazy blue line. The sun climbed higher, its warmth seeping into her skin, but she felt a chill that had nothing to do with the temperature.

A flock of seagulls wheeled overhead, their cries carrying on the salt-tinged breeze. Anna watched them circle and dive, moving in perfect synchronization.

She thought of Beth, her sister's presence both a comfort and a source of anxiety. The camaraderie between Casper and Waldo, for all its friction, spoke of a connection she struggled to form.

She frowned. "Get it together, Gabriel."

Her scowl deepened as she shook her head, trying to pull herself back together. But these were the stray thoughts the others didn't see. They didn't see the weeks of sleepless nights, the tightening in her stomach at every new danger.

She'd lived a life trying to protect others. She now focused on protecting her baby sister, but in it all Beth had lost her husband, her two children. Who even knew for sure if they were still alive?

Anna owed it to Beth to try and find out...

Still, another part of her felt as if she were in constant motion. If she didn't keep swimming, eventually, she'd drown.

As she tried to force herself to focus, her mind wandered anyway. Had she ever cared about something—someone—as much as Beth cared about her family?

Anna had always known she'd signed up for a lonely life, and she hated to admit how spending time with her sister—her own flesh and blood—was only heightening the feeling...

She took a deep breath, steeling herself. This mission was too important for doubts or distractions. She squared her shoulders and strode purposefully toward the main cabin, her footsteps echoing on the deck.

Chapter 5

As she entered, the others looked up expectantly. Casper was leaning against the bar, his posture tense. Beth perched nervously on the edge of a plush leather sofa, while Waldo sprawled in an armchair, his legs dangling over one arm. Waldo, she noticed, had spiked his black hair, making him look like a porcupine, and he had a new tattoo on his left arm...

It was the exact same bone frog tattoo Anna had.

She stared at it.

He beamed at her. "Like it? My own design."

She approached Waldo slowly. As she drew nearer, his shit-eating grin only got bigger. "Ah, come on, now... Don't get all upset. It's just temporary ink."

She glanced down, up again. "No. It isn't."

He winced. "Fair... so I was drunk."

"You need to cover that," she said simply. Her voice left no room for argument.

Casper sighed. "What did he do this time?"

Anna pointed. Casper's eyes followed, and then he blinked. He released a slow whistling sound and clasped his hands over his eyes.

"Tell him, Casper. Tell him why he needs to remove that."

"It's a tattoo," Waldo muttered, sitting up a bit in his chair now, no longer looking so relaxed. "Can't remove it."

"I can," Anna growled.

"Psh—what? You gonna cut my arm off?" A pause... "Anna... Anna, hang on, you're not going to cut my arm off, are you?"

"Casper?" she growled, looking away. "I won't look at that. He didn't earn it."

"What's the big deal?" Waldo pleaded, the spiky-headed pain-in-the-ass making a whining sound like a chastised child.

Casper approached, playing the role of peace-broker.

The ex–special operator stepped between Anna and Waldo, his hands raised placatingly. "Alright, let's all take a breath here." He turned to Waldo, his voice stern. "That tattoo is a SEAL symbol. It's sacred to those who've earned it. You need to cover it up."

Waldo's face fell, realization dawning. "Oh... shit. I didn't think—"

"No, you didn't," Anna cut in, her voice cold.

"You're not mad at *me*," Waldo insisted. "You're made at this giant floating hotel."

"I'm pretty sure I'm mad at you."

Beth watched the exchange with wide eyes, clearly uncomfortable with the tension. "Maybe we could just... put a bandage over it?" she suggested hesitantly.

Anna's jaw clenched, but she nodded curtly. "Fine. But if I see it again, Strange, we're going to have a problem. Understood?"

Waldo swallowed hard, nodding vigorously. "Crystal clear. I'll keep it covered. Scout's honor." He mimed a salute, then winced as Anna's glare intensified.

Casper cleared his throat. "Now that's settled, let's focus on the mission." He spread a map across the low table in the center of the cabin to brief Waldo. "Our route takes us across the Caspian Sea to Türkmenbaşy. From there, we head inland."

Anna leaned over the map, her earlier anger giving way to focused concentration. "The port will be heavily guarded. We'll need a solid cover story and ironclad documentation."

Waldo perked up, eager to move past his faux pas. "Already on it. I've got us set up as a group of wealthy eco-tourists. Paperwork's all in order, and I've even set up a fake social media trail to back it up."

Anna nodded grudgingly. "Good. Once we're in the country, we'll need to move fast. The compound is here." She pointed to a spot in the foothills of the Köpetdag Mountains. "Heavily fortified, but our intel suggests the Albino will be there for the next week."

Beth shifted uncomfortably. "And... what about Tony and Sarah?"

Anna softened slightly as she looked at her sister. "If the Albino has them, we'll find out. But remember, Beth, this is reconnaissance first. We're not equipped for a full extraction."

Beth nodded, her face pale but determined. "I understand. I just... need to know if they're alive."

Anna squeezed her sister's shoulder gently. "We'll find out. I promise."

Waldo cleared his throat. "Not to be a downer, but what's our exit strategy? Turkmenistan isn't exactly known for its open borders." He paused and held up a finger. "And like we agreed, I'm staying on the ship. Right?"

No one answered.

"Riiight?" he pressed a bit harder.

Casper and Anna didn't reply. Instead, Casper answered Waldo's earlier question.

Casper folded his arms across his chest, his expression grim. "Exit strategy is where things get tricky. Once we're in, we're essentially on our own. No cavalry coming if things go south."

Anna kept her eyes fixed on the map. "We'll have a seventy-two-hour window. If we haven't achieved our objective by then, we abort and make for the extraction point here." She tapped a spot on the coastline, about a hundred miles north of Türkmenbaşy.

Waldo leaned in, squinting at the map. "That's... pretty much the middle of nowhere. How are we supposed to get picked up?"

"We don't," Anna replied flatly. "We'll have to commandeer a boat and make our way back across the Caspian."

Beth's eyes widened. "Commandeer? You mean steal?"

Anna met her sister's gaze steadily. "If it comes to that, yes. But let's hope it doesn't."

Casper coughed. "There's one more thing we need to discuss. Weapons."

Anna's eyebrow raised slightly. "I thought you had that covered."

Casper nodded. "I do, but there's been a... complication. Our contact in Türkmenbaşy can only smuggle in a limited amount. We'll have to be selective."

Anna's jaw tightened. "How limited?"

"Two sidearms, one rifle, and a handful of grenades," Casper replied. "Plus whatever we can conceal on our persons."

Waldo piped up, "Don't forget my toys! I've got some nifty little gadgets that might come in handy."

Anna shot him a withering look. "Your 'toys' better not get us killed, Strange."

Waldo held up his hands defensively. "Hey, when have my inventions ever let you down?"

"Couple of months ago," Anna shot back without missing a beat.

Waldo winced. "Okay, fair point. But I've improved since then!"

Casper interjected before the argument could escalate. "We'll take what we can get. Anna, you and I will carry the sidearms. I'll take the rifle."

Anna agreed. "Beth, you stick close to me at all times. Waldo, you're our eyes and ears from the ship. Monitor communications, satellite feeds, anything you can get your hands on."

Waldo saluted. "Aye, aye, captain."

Anna ignored him, turning back to the group. "Any questions?"

Beth raised her hand halfway. "What... what do we do if we find them? Tony and Sarah, I mean."

A heavy silence fell over the cabin. Anna met her sister's gaze at last. "If we find them, we make a plan to come back and get them out." She turned to Casper. "And you," she said, "make sure this neon sign of a boat doesn't get us all sunk."

Casper sighed but gave a single shrug. "In Turkmenistan, it's not the sinking I'm worried about."

"What are you worried about?" Beth asked.

Casper spoke, his voice low and serious. "The country's crawling with secret police, informants, and surveillance. Every phone call, every email, every conversation in public could be monitored. Trust no one outside this room."

Anna motioned agreement. "And even within the country, there are invisible lines you don't cross. Regions controlled by different factions, tribal territories where outsiders aren't welcome. One wrong step, and we could disappear without a trace."

Waldo let out a low whistle. "Sounds like a real paradise. Remind me again why I agreed to this?"

Casper growled. "Because the payout is worth the risk."

Anna's eyes narrowed at the mention of money, but she let it slide. Now wasn't the time for that discussion. "We have three days to prepare once we reach Türkmenbaşy. Learn your cover stories inside and out. Memorize the maps. And be ready for anything."

Beth concentrated on the papers laid out on the table, determination creasing her eyes.

As the group dispersed to their respective tasks, Anna lingered by the map. Her fingers traced the route they would take, each bend and twist representing countless potential dangers. The weight of responsibility settled heavily on her shoulders.

She glanced out the cabin window, watching the endless expanse of the Caspian Sea roll by. Somewhere beyond that horizon lay Turkmenistan, and with it, the answers they sought.

The yacht cut through the waves, carrying them inexorably toward danger.

Chapter 6

For three days they'd tracked the luxury yacht.

Three days the ship had gone unmolested through the vast expanse of the Caspian Sea, keeping to the coast, making stops... It took the path of a tourist vessel.

But Sergeant Kovac knew better.

She was back in town.

After what he'd seen on that dock in Astrakhan, he recognized the work.

The water had shifted from deep azure to a murky green-brown as they neared the Turkmenistan coast. Salt-laden night air whipped across the deck, carrying the faint scent of desert and oil refineries.

The assault boat sliced through the inky waters. Sergeant Kovac gripped his rifle tightly, eyes straining to pierce the darkness ahead. The low thrum of muffled engines vibrated through the hull, a steady pulse beneath his feet.

Ten other figures crouched low in the boat, their black tactical gear rendering them nearly invisible against the dark. No one spoke. No one needed to. They'd rehearsed this a dozen times. Each man knew his role, his position, his objectives.

Kovac allowed his gaze to sweep over his team. Faces obscured by balaclavas and night vision goggles, they were more shadow than human. Only the occasional glint of a weapon or piece of equipment betrayed their presence.

The salty spray stung his exposed skin as they cut through a particularly choppy section. Kovac tasted brine on his lips. His mind drifted momentarily to earlier that evening, to the briefing that had set this operation in motion.

"Anna Gabriel, the Guardian Angel, is coming back to Europe," the intelligence officer had said, his voice tinged with excitement and fear in equal measure. "She should've known to stay clear. And now it's our job to secure the cargo."

Kovac had heard the stories, of course. They all had. Anna Gabriel was a ghost, a myth, a boogeyman that kept even hardened operatives awake at night. But ghosts didn't bleed. And myths couldn't die.

A pinprick of light appeared on the horizon, growing steadily larger. Their target. The yacht loomed in the distance, a gleaming white behemoth against the starlit sky. Its deck lights blazed, creating a halo of illumination on the water around it.

Kovac raised a fist, signaling the team to ready themselves. Weapons were checked one final time. Grappling hooks were prepared. The boat's engines dropped to an almost imperceptible purr as they entered the yacht's radar shadow.

As they drew closer, Kovac could make out details of the vessel. Its sleek lines and ostentatious size spoke of obscene wealth. The kind of wealth that often attracted trouble. Or in this case, invited it.

The assault boat glided to a stop alongside the yacht's hull, bumpers deployed silently to prevent any telltale sounds. Kovac nodded to his second-in-command. In one fluid motion, grappling hooks were launched, catching on the yacht's railing above.

Kovac took a deep breath, steadying himself for what was to come. Anna Gabriel might be legend, but legends fell to bullets just the same as any man. And he had twelve highly trained operatives ready to test that theory.

With a final hand signal, Kovac began to climb. The hunt was on.

Chapter 7

Anna woke with a start. She peered out the porthole window toward the distant specks of light. *Far too few lights*, she thought. As if the city were struggling to illuminate the shore. She remembered pictures she'd once seen of North Korea, and how the country appeared to be a black void at night compared to its brightly lit neighbors.

She always woke early. Sleep was elusive. The same as peace. The same as calm.

It was why she stayed on the move. Now, her senses were heightened. Alert once more.

The yacht's engines had dropped to a low purr, barely discernible over the lapping of waves. They were close to shore, preparing to dock in Türkmenbaşy. But that wasn't what had woken her.

Anna pressed her ear to the cabin door, listening intently. At first, she heard nothing but the usual creaks and groans of a ship at sea. Then—there. A soft thud from above, followed by the faintest scrape of metal on metal.

Hushed movements outside her door but no voices.

No voices...

Shit.

Egress. Now.

Where? Beth—upstairs. Safe. Two doors—bulletproof. Anna had made sure. Beth would be safe.

So where?

They weren't here for Beth. They knew what they were doing. They were here for her, weren't they?

Anna's mind raced, calculating her options in milliseconds. The door was out of the question—a tactical error that would alert the intruders to her position. Her eyes darted once again to the porthole, a circular window barely large enough for her compact frame.

With practiced efficiency, Anna retrieved a small device from her go-bag—a glass breaker, its tungsten carbide tip designed for silent shattering. She pressed it against the thick glass, applying steady pressure. A spiderweb of cracks spread outward, contained by the rubber seal around the porthole's edge.

Anna held her breath, listening intently for any reaction from outside her cabin. Nothing. The faint shuffling continued, oblivious to her actions.

With agonizing slowness, she removed the fractured glass piece by piece, laying each shard noiselessly on the carpeted floor. The salty night air rushed in.

Anna squeezed through the opening, her lithe body contorting to fit the narrow space. Her fingers found purchase on the yacht's smooth hull, slick with sea spray. She clung to the porthole's edge, muscles straining as she suspended herself outside the vessel.

The water below was an inky void, its surface barely visible in the predawn gloom. Türkmenbaşy's meager lights flickered on the horizon, offering no salvation. Anna's options were limited—she couldn't drop into the sea. And climbing?

Nothing above, just slick metal.

She was stuck.

So she waited, fingers white-knuckled on the porthole's rim, body pressed flat against the cold metal of the hull. The gentle rocking of the yacht threatened to dislodge her precarious grip. Each passing second felt like an eternity as Anna strained her ears, listening for any clue to the intruders' movements.

A bead of sweat trickled down her temple despite the chill. Her arms began to burn with the effort of maintaining her position. But she remained motionless, her breath slow and controlled. She had weathered worse conditions, endured greater hardships. This was merely another test of will.

The sound of the waves below masked any noise coming from within the yacht. Anna closed her eyes, focusing her other senses. The slight vibration of footsteps transmitted through metal. The almost imperceptible change in air pressure as a door opened somewhere above.

She waited, muscles coiled like springs, ready to act at a moment's notice but biding her time. Anna Gabriel, the Guardian Angel, was nothing if not patient.

But then came the scream.

Beth's scream.

***

GUARDIAN FOR HIRE

Sergeant Kovac's breath came in shallow bursts, muffled by his balaclava. Sweat beaded on his forehead, threatening to drip into his eyes. He blinked rapidly, willing his vision to remain clear. The narrow corridor of the luxury yacht felt claustrophobic, the air thick with tension and the acrid smell of gun oil.

Eight of his men crowded behind him, their black tactical gear melding into the shadows. Only the occasional glint of a weapon or night vision goggles betrayed their presence. They were wound tight, ready to unleash violence at his command.

Three others were upstairs, breaching the reinforced doors they'd spotted on the upper deck.

Captain Yevgeny knelt before Kovac, his usually crisp white uniform now rumpled and stained with sweat. The captain's weathered face was pale, his eyes wide with terror as he stared down the barrel of Kovac's pistol.

"I swear," Yevgeny whimpered, his accent thickening with fear. "This is her room. The woman you seek."

Kovac's jaw clenched beneath his mask. He reached into a pocket with his free hand, withdrawing a folded photograph. With a flick of his wrist, he snapped it open, shoving it under the captain's nose.

"This woman?" Kovac growled, his voice low and menacing.

The photograph showed a woman in her mid-thirties, her features sharp and angular. Piercing green eyes stared out from the image, seeming to challenge the viewer. A distinctive streak of white cut through her dark hair, adding to her striking appearance. The set of her jaw and the intensity of her gaze spoke of a hardened soldier, someone who had seen more than their fair share of combat. There was something unnerving about those eyes, though. Something in them that stood out... or perhaps something that *should* have been there, but was missing.

Yevgeny nodded vigorously, his chin quivering. "Yes, yes! That's her. This is her cabin. I swear it on my life!"

Kovac's eyes narrowed behind his goggles. He gestured to the door with a jerk of his head. Two of his men moved forward, flanking the entrance. One produced a small device—a fiber optic camera—and carefully slid it under the door.

Tense seconds ticked by as the operator manipulated the camera, scanning the room's interior. Kovac watched the man's body language, waiting for any sign of what they'd found.

Finally, the operator looked up, shaking his head slightly. Kovac felt a surge of frustration and anger. The room was empty.

He turned back to Yevgeny, grabbing a fistful of the captain's uniform and yanking him close. "Where is she?" he snarled.

Yevgeny's eyes darted wildly, panic evident in every line of his face. "I-I don't know! She should be there! Maybe... maybe she's with her sister? The blonde woman, one deck up?"

Kovac released the captain, his mind racing. He pressed a finger to his earpiece. "Team Two, status?"

"Sir, we've breached the upper cabin," came the reply. "One female occupant secured. Blonde, early thirties. She's not our target."

Kovac cursed under his breath. Gabriel had slipped through their fingers somehow. But how? Where could she have gone?

He turned back to Captain Yevgeny, who still knelt trembling on the floor. Kovac crouched down, getting eye-level with the terrified man.

"You've been very helpful, Captain," Kovac said softly. "But I'm afraid your usefulness has come to an end. Do you know anything about poetry?"

Kovac's left eye twitched. He could feel his blood pumping, his excitement rising. He licked at the corner of his lip and released a slow exhale.

"P-p-please," the captain whimpered.

Kovac tilted his head slightly, pulling down his balaclava to see more clearly. He liked it when they begged.

Poetry in motion.

For a moment, nothing else mattered.

It had always been Kovac's greatest weakness... this... hyper-fixation. He lost sight of it all. His attention narrowed to a tunnel.

It was the reason they'd demoted him. The reason his wife had left... Well, that and what he'd done to her face.

Kovac's eyes gleamed with a twisted light as he regarded the trembling captain. His mind drifted to the elegant brutality that awaited, the graceful arc of blood, the symphony of breaking bones. To Kovac, violence was an art form, and he its devoted practitioner.

"There's poetry in death, Captain," Kovac murmured, his voice taking on an almost dreamy quality. "The interplay of muscle and sinew, the delicate dance of nerves firing their last. It's... beautiful."

He remembered his days in the Spetsnaz, where he had first discovered his talent for dealing death. Each mission, each kill, had been a stanza in an ever-evolving epic. The crack of a sniper rifle echoing across Chechen mountains. The wet gurgle of a sentry's last breath in the forests of Georgia. The muffled thump of bodies hitting snow-covered ground outside a compound in Kazakhstan.

Kovac's fingers twitched, recalling the precise pressure needed to snap a man's neck. He could almost feel the captain's pulse beneath his hands, the frantic flutter of a heart pumping its last.

"Did you know," Kovac continued, his voice soft and intimate, "that the human body contains roughly five liters of blood? When it spills, it moves like liquid rubies. The patterns it makes... exquisite. Like calligraphy written by angels."

He leaned closer to the captain, drinking in the man's terror. "I've spent years perfecting my craft, studying the human form, learning its weaknesses, its vulnerabilities. Each kill is a verse, each mission a canto in my magnum opus."

Kovac's mind raced with possibilities. Would he make it quick, a clean slice across the throat, letting the captain's lifeblood paint the pristine white of his uniform? Or something slower, more intricate? Perhaps he would demonstrate the delicate art of pressure points, showing how the human body could be turned against itself, nerves singing in agony until the sweet release of death.

"P-please," the captain sobbed, "I have a family..."

Kovac smiled, a cold, reptilian expression devoid of warmth or mercy. "As do we all, Captain. But in this moment, you are my canvas, my instrument. Together, we will create something... transcendent."

As Kovac prepared to begin his gruesome work, a scream pierced the night—high, terrified, and distinctly female. It came from above, where his men had already secured the blonde woman.

Kovac's head snapped up, his reverie broken.

He scowled deeply. "Where *is she*?" he demanded a final time.

"I don't know! She was in her room!" the captain moaned.

In one smooth motion, Kovac pulled a tactical pen from a pocket on his vest. With his other hand, he grabbed a fistful of the captain's thinning hair, yanking his head back to expose his throat.

"You're a liar," Kovac whispered. He brought the pen to Yevgeny's forehead, using the sharp tip to slowly carve letters into the captain's flesh. Blood welled up, trickling down the man's face. "Don't... move."

"I'm not lying! Agh—please! NO!" Yevgeny cried out, his eyes wide with terror. Kovac finished his grim work, then paused, admiring the message he'd left.

Without warning, Kovac plunged the pen deep into the side of Yevgeny's neck, finding the carotid artery with practiced precision. Blood sprayed in a crimson arc as Kovac wrenched the pen free.

He watched dispassionately as the light faded from the captain's eyes, observing the spasms that wracked the dying man's body. It was, in its own way, a kind of poetry—the final throes of life, played out in twitching muscles and fading gasps.

As Yevgeny's body slumped to the floor, Kovac stood, wiping the bloodied pen on the captain's white uniform. He turned to his team, his voice cold and determined.

"Find her," he ordered. "Breach the door. Now!"

Three of the soldiers behind him moved. All of them ex-KGB or Spetsnaz. All of them highly trained.

The three soldiers moved forward in tight formation, their rifles raised and ready. Each step was deliberate and silent, their boots barely making a sound on the carpeted floor of the corridor. The faint scent of blood from Yevgeny's body still lingered.

Kovac followed them, his movements purposeful. His mind was already shifting from the captain to his true target—Anna Gabriel. Every part of him burned to track her down, to feel the thrill of the hunt as he cornered her like prey. He knew what she was capable of. He had read every report, studied every tactic she'd used in operations around the globe. He relished it—the challenge she presented. This wasn't another hapless victim or undisciplined thug. Anna Gabriel was a soldier, a killer... an artist in her own way.

But Kovac believed himself superior.

As they approached her cabin door, one of the soldiers crouched low and affixed a small explosive charge to the lock. His fingers worked quickly, efficiently, securing it in place with adhesive strips before stepping back into position. Kovac motioned for the others to take cover on each side of the corridor.

A low hum filled the air as the charge gave off its final alert—a sharp series of quick beeps—and then came the blast.

The door flew inward with a deafening crack, splinters and shards of metal scattering across the room beyond. Smoke swirled in the corridor as Kovac signaled his men forward with two quick gestures.

They poured into the cabin, sweeping their weapons left and right as they cleared each corner with precision. The room was neat but unoccupied—the bed untouched save for precisely placed pieces of glass, no signs of movement or struggle. The porthole stood open, its glass shattered neatly around its rim.

Kovac's lip curled as he moved into the room behind his men, his sharp eyes scanning every detail. She had escaped through the porthole—no doubt about it—but where could she have gone? His mind shuffled through possibilities as he leaned out of the opening slightly, peering downward into the darkness below.

The waves made it hard to distinguish any shapes or movement against the hull of the yacht, but something caught his attention—a faint smudge on the slick surface just below the porthole's edge. His gloved hand brushed against it—a subtle smear of oil mixed with seawater.

"She didn't drop," he said aloud in Russian to no one in particular. "She climbed."

One of his soldiers stepped forward, voice clipped and professional through his mask. "Thermal scan detected no heat signature on this side of the hull."

"She wouldn't linger," Kovac replied coldly. "She's smarter than that." His hand tightened briefly into a fist before he turned back to his men and barked out an order. "Check all exterior decks—every inch! I want her found now."

The soldiers nodded in unison.

Kovac exhaled slowly, forcing himself to suppress his rising irritation—even admiration. But he wouldn't let it last long; failure wasn't an option tonight—not when it came to her.

He hesitated, looking through the window once more.

But *how* had she climbed? There were no handholds... no footholds. No...

His eyes widened in horror.

"Back!" he screamed. "Back!"

Too late.

A shadow unfolded from under the bed. She'd been absent when they'd checked with the camera, but then she had reentered the room before they'd breeched. So simple.

So effective.

And now, it was like watching a pool of darkness spread from some sulfur pit. The *thing* crawled, skittered from under the bed, moving fast.

She wasn't stronger than most of the muscled men. She wasn't larger.

But she was faster. Dear God was she fast.

His scream died on his lips as the Guardian Angel sliced the necks of two of his toughest operators before he'd even cried his first warning. Then all mayhem broke out.

The closed quarters was a whirlwind of violence. The Guardian moved like liquid shadow, her body twisting and contorting in ways that seemed to defy physics. She flowed between the soldiers, her knife flashing in the dim light, finding gaps in body armor and slicing through flesh with surgical precision.

One of the remaining soldiers managed to raise his rifle, but Anna was already in motion. She dropped low, sweeping his legs out from under him. As he fell, she grabbed his Kevlar vest, using his own momentum to swing him around as a human shield. A burst of gunfire from another soldier peppered the falling man's back, the impact jolting Anna's arms but leaving her unscathed.

In one fluid motion, she shrugged the dead man's vest off and onto her own torso, just as another soldier opened fire. The bullets thudded against the Kevlar, the force driving the air from her lungs but saving her life. Anna's hand shot out, fingers wrapping around the wrist of the shooter. She twisted sharply, bones cracking as the rifle clattered to the floor.

Kovac watched in a mix of horror and awe as Anna decimated his team. She moved with a grace that bordered on supernatural, each action twisting seamlessly into the next. A punch became an elbow strike, became a throw, became a lethal knife thrust. It was like watching a deadly ballet.

As the last soldier fell, Anna's eyes locked with Kovac's. For a heartbeat, time seemed to stand still. Then her hand moved, unhooking a grenade from the vest she wore. With lightning speed, she pulled the pin and hurled the entire vest toward Kovac.

Kovac's survival instincts kicked in. He dove backwards, his body twisting in midair as he crashed through the porthole. The sharp edges of the broken glass tore at his clothes and skin as he plummeted toward the dark waters below.

The explosion rocked the yacht, the confined space of the cabin amplifying the blast. Heat and shrapnel burst outward, missing Kovac by mere inches as he hit the water with a resounding splash.

As he surfaced, gasping for air, Kovac looked up at the smoldering hole where the porthole had been. Smoke billowed out, obscuring his view of the cabin. But for a brief moment, he thought he saw a silhouette framed against the flames—a figure with a distinctive streak of white in her dark hair, watching him with calculating eyes.

Then she was gone, leaving Kovac treading water in the inky blackness of the Caspian Sea, the taste of defeat bitter on his tongue.

Chapter 8

Anna had no time to celebrate. Screaming upstairs. Beth. She was already moving, but then the sound of the crackling radio caught her attention.

She heard a voice shouting on the other end.

Anna snatched up the radio, her fingers slick with blood—some hers, most not. The voice on the other end was frantic, demanding answers in rapid-fire Russian.

"Kovac! Kovac, chto, chert voz'mi, proizoshlo?"

Anna's lips curled as she keyed the mic. "I'm afraid Kovac can't come to the phone right now," she replied in flawless Russian, her voice low and controlled. "But I'd be happy to take a message."

There was a moment of stunned silence. Then the voice returned, anger and fear warring for dominance in its tone. "Who is this? Where is Kovac?"

"Kovac is taking an unscheduled swim," Anna said coolly. "Now, let's talk about something more important. Do you want to live?"

The voice sputtered, indignation overriding caution. "You bitch! Do you have any idea who you're dealing with? We'll—"

"Don't hurt the girl upstairs," Anna cut in, her tone sharp as a blade. "Don't hurt anyone. Those are my terms if you want to walk away from this."

The voice on the radio shifted tactics, panic creeping in at the edges. "You're in no position to make demands! We have hostages. We have—"

Anna lowered the radio, letting the threats fade into background noise. She cocked her head, listening intently. The yacht creaked and groaned around her, but beneath that, she could hear movement. Footsteps above, the scrape of boots on deck. Shouting, muffled but angry.

She raised the radio again, cutting off the stream of threats. "Is my sister anywhere near you?"

There was a pause, then a reply. "She's on the bed. And we'll keep her there... Do you understand? You better do as we say or we'll hurt her—bad!"

Anna's jaw clenched. She could picture Beth, terrified and alone, surrounded by armed men.

Those footsteps.

One... two? Three.

Three men.

She needed noise, now.

Lots of noise.

Anna's voice remained steady as she spoke into the radio. "Let's be clear about something. You're not in control here. You're not the hunter. You're prey that doesn't realize it's already dead."

Meaningless words. Words that didn't resonate with her. They were just tools.

But the man on the other end didn't know it. Blood dripped from her wrist where she gripped the radio.

She paused, letting her words sink in. Then she continued, her tone precise. "I've killed more men than you've met in your entire life. I've toppled governments, eliminated terrorist cells, and walked away from war zones that would have you pissing your pants. So when I say I'm going to kill every last one of you if you harm a hair on my sister's head, you'd better believe it."

The man sputtered, his voice rising in pitch and volume. "You think you scare me? You're nothing! We—"

Anna cut him off. She needed louder. Angrier. "Professionals? Please. I've seen mall cops with better tactics. You couldn't even secure a yacht properly. And now more than half your team is dead or dying. Face it, you're out of your league."

The man's composure cracked. He began shouting, his words becoming a stream of profanity and threats. "I'll gut your sister myself! I'll make you watch as I—"

Loud enough. Perfect.

Anna tuned out his words, focusing instead on the sound of his voice. Not through the radio, but through the ceiling above her. As he ranted, she could pinpoint his location, tracking his movements as he paced back and forth.

Calmly, she set down the radio, cutting off his tirade mid-sentence. She reached for one of the fallen soldiers, retrieving his tactical rifle. The weapon felt familiar in her hands as she checked the magazine.

Three sets of footsteps. Her sister on the bed.

Moving... not Waldo or Casper. Not an ally if moving. No. Men in control. Men on the prowl. She'd heard foreign background voices over the radio. Two. Gruff. Russian. Three assailants, as she'd suspected. Three sets of feet. Close enough to hear over the radio. Now one loud enough to locate.

Easy.

She'd memorized the blueprints of the yacht before agreeing to travel, anyway. She'd double-memorized them when placing her sister in the upstairs room.

Anna took a deep breath, centering herself. Then, in one swift motion, she raised the rifle and fired three controlled bursts through the ceiling. The gunfire was deafening in the confined space, but she ignored it, listening intently.

Two distinct thuds followed, the sound of bodies hitting the floor. But not three. Anna's eyes narrowed. She adjusted her aim slightly to the left—a shuffling sound. She hesitated, listened. A faint whimper. She fired another burst.

A third thump echoed from above, followed by silence.

Anna lowered the rifle, her expression grim.

She dropped the gun, letting it clatter to the floor, and then she broke into a jog, stepping over the corpses as if they were tire obstacles on a training course.

She raced up the stairs to the upper deck.

"Anna!" Beth's voice was calling. "Anna! We're in here. We're okay—Anna, where are you?"

Anna didn't reply. No sense attracting any further attackers.

But she redoubled her pace. As she ran, she spotted the small boarding vessel *thumping* against the hull of their larger ship. Bingo.

They had their boat to shore.

Plan. Pivot. Plan. Pivot.

This was the rhythm of any op.

And they were already in the thick of it. A closed nation awaited just a mile away, the shoreline winking back at her like a shark's eyes in the deep, waiting for her to come too close.

Chapter 9

The plans had changed. It was Casper who'd made the call, as the four of them now crowded into their stolen speedboat, racing away from the yacht.

Anna suspected that her old partner-in-crime felt guilty he'd been pinned down during the raid. He'd managed to dispatch a couple of shooters who'd broken off from the others—they'd nearly shot him in his hammock below decks—but his expression was intense as he eyed the Kazakhstan coast.

The speedboat cut through the choppy waters, its powerful engine roaring as they raced away from the yacht. The night air was heavy with salt and diesel fumes, stinging Anna's eyes as she scanned the horizon. The distant lights of Kazakhstan's coast glimmered like a string of pearls against the inky blackness.

Casper hunched over the controls, his weathered face etched with lines of concentration. The boat's wake frothed white behind them, a temporary scar on the dark surface of the Caspian Sea. Beth huddled in the center, clutching a waterproof duffel bag to her chest, her blonde hair whipping wildly in the wind. Waldo clung to the side railing, his face a nauseating shade of green as he battled seasickness.

"We're changing course," Casper shouted over the engine's roar. "Landing in Turkmenistan now would be suicide. Too much heat after that shootout."

Anna's eyes narrowed. "Where to, then?"

Casper jerked his head toward the distant lights. "Kazakhstan. I've got a contact there—Dastan Bek. Former Turkmenistan special forces, now works as a fixer. He can get us across the border quietly."

The boat crested a particularly large wave, sending spray cascading over them. Waldo retched over the side, earning a sympathetic pat on the back from Beth.

"And you trust this Bek?" Anna asked, her voice skeptical.

Casper's jaw tightened. "As much as I trust anyone in this game. He's got a vested interest in keeping us alive—we're his meal ticket to a comfortable retirement."

Anna nodded, processing the information. She thought through contingencies, calculating risks and potential outcomes. She'd already discarded the worry about last night's attack, deciding to examine it like a coroner studying a corpse on a metal table.

Long ago, she'd given up on trying to find *fear* in things. But lessons? Lessons prepared her for future tasks. She frowned. "The name Kovac... mean anything to you?" she asked suddenly.

Casper's hands tightened on the wheel, his knuckles whitening. He cursed under his breath before answering. "You heard that name last night?"

"One of the assholes who got away. Weird twitch."

"Yeah. I heard it. Hitman. Ex-Spetsnaz. Psychotic bastard with a reputation for... creative kills."

"He led the team on the yacht," Anna said flatly. "He was looking for me."

Casper's head snapped around, his eyes wide. "You're sure?"

Anna nodded grimly. "He took an unscheduled swim, but I doubt that's the last we've seen of him."

Casper muttered another curse, this one more colorful than the last. "That complicates things. Kovac's not the type to let a target go. He'll be after us with everything he's got."

The coastline grew larger as they approached, details emerging from the darkness. Rocky cliffs gave way to a narrow strip of beach, beyond which Anna could make out the outlines of weathered buildings and rusted cranes—the remnants of the oil boom.

Waldo, still a sickly color that matched the dye he sometimes used in his hair, looked over at Casper. "Who is this Bek guy, anyway?" He looked ready to add something else, but then held up a finger, vomiting over the rail.

Anna held back a smirk. It wouldn't have been professional. Beth made a soothing sound, rubbing the man's shoulder in small circular motions.

"I told you."

"But what's the plan?" Waldo insisted, rubbing at his lips with the back of his hand, a string of drool trailing. "I'm not cut out for this. I was supposed to stay on the boat, remember?"

Casper sighed. "You'll be fine. Besides... Bek's taking us in the entourage of a billionaire."

At the word *billionaire,* Waldo perked up, looking much healthier all of a sudden.

As the speedboat neared the shore, Casper cut the engine, letting them drift the final distance. The sudden silence was jarring after the constant roar. Waves lapped gently against the hull as Casper explained their new plan.

"Bek's got connections with the Turkmen elite," he began, his voice low. "There's a falconry event in Ashgabat next week—big deal for the oligarchs and government officials. Bek's arranged for us to enter the country as part of a billionaire's entourage."

Anna raised an eyebrow. "Falcon trainers?"

Casper nodded. "Elite falconers from Kazakhstan, bringing prized birds for the event. It's the perfect cover—these guys are used to crossing borders with minimal scrutiny. Their birds are worth more than most people make in a lifetime."

Beth's eyes widened. "But... we don't know anything about falcons."

"You don't have to," Casper replied. "Bek's got everything arranged—fake credentials, costumes, even a few trained birds to sell the act. We just need to keep our mouths shut and look the part."

Waldo, still looking queasy, piped up. "And who's this billionaire we're supposed to be working for?"

"Gurbanguly Atayev," Casper said. "Oil tycoon, friend of the president. The kind of man who can make problems disappear with a phone call."

Anna's mind raced, processing the information. It was a bold plan, audacious even. But in a country as tightly controlled as Turkmenistan, audacity might be their best bet.

"What's our window?" she asked.

"Three days," Casper replied. "We cross the border tomorrow night, make our way to Ashgabat, then have forty-eight hours to locate the Albino and extract any intel on Beth's family."

Beth clutched the duffel bag tighter. "And if we can't find him in time?"

Casper's expression hardened. "Then we abort. No exceptions. Overstaying our welcome in Turkmenistan is a death sentence."

The boat bumped gently against the shore, the keel scraping sand. Casper killed the lights, plunging them into near-total darkness. In the distance, Anna could make out the faint outline of a vehicle—their ride, presumably.

As they began to disembark, Waldo grabbed Anna's arm. His face was serious, all traces of seasickness gone. "Anna, listen. I've done some digging on Turkmenistan. It's… it's bad. Really bad. Makes North Korea look like Disneyland."

Anna nodded grimly. "I know. We've been over this."

"W-we have?"

"Pretty sure you were in the room for it, Waldo."

"Well, I wasn't listening. But look, the whole country's like something out of Orwell's—"

But Casper cut him off. "There," he said, pointing to a small cove nestled between two rocky outcroppings. "We'll make landfall there. Bek should have transport waiting."

As they neared the shore, Anna scanned the beach, searching for any signs of movement or hidden threats. The cove was deserted, save for a battered pickup truck parked at the edge of the sand.

Anna was the first one out, water splashing up to her thighs as she dragged the boat further onto the beach.

"Move fast," she ordered, helping Beth out of the boat. "We're exposed here."

Waldo stumbled onto the sand, still looking green. "I think I left my stomach somewhere back in the Caspian," he groaned.

"You'll live," Anna said curtly. She turned to Casper. "Where's this contact of yours?"

As if on cue, the pickup truck's headlights flashed twice. A figure emerged from the shadows, approaching with a casual gait that belied the tension in the air.

"Casper, my friend!" the man called out in heavily accented English. "It's been too long."

Casper grinned, though Anna noted the wariness in his eyes. "Dastan. Good to see you're still breathing."

Dastan Bek was a stocky man in his late forties with close-cropped salt-and-pepper hair and a neatly trimmed beard. His weathered face spoke of years spent in harsh conditions, but his eyes were sharp and alert.

"And you brought friends," Dastan observed, his gaze lingering on Anna. "The famous Guardian Angel, I presume?"

Anna's hand twitched toward her concealed weapon. "You know who I am?"

Dastan raised his hands in a placating gesture. "In my line of work, it pays to know the players. Your reputation precedes you."

"Let's skip the pleasantries. " Anna replied coolly. "Can you get us across the border?"

Dastan's eyes narrowed slightly, but he nodded. "For the right price, I can get you to the moon. But first, we need to move. This beach isn't as deserted as it looks."

As if to emphasize his point, a distant engine rumbled to life. Headlights appeared on the cliff road above, moving in their direction.

"Damn it," Casper muttered. "Kovac?"

"Unlikely," Dastan replied, already heading toward his truck. "But equally unfriendly. Border patrol. They're not known for their hospitality."

Anna herded Beth and Waldo toward the vehicle. "Move. Now."

As they piled into the battered pickup truck, Anna assessed their options. The approaching headlights grew brighter, illuminating the beach in harsh white light.

"Dastan," she snapped, "how far to the border?"

The fixer gunned the engine, tires spinning in the loose sand before gaining ground. "Two hours, give or take. But we've got a problem—that patrol will radio ahead. Every checkpoint from here to Turkmenistan will be on high alert."

Casper cursed, his face grim in the dim glow of the dashboard lights. "We need a diversion."

Anna agreed, a plan already forming. "The boat," she said. "Waldo, tell me you brought some of your toys."

The hacker's face lit up, a manic grin spreading across his features. "Oh, you know I did. What did you have in mind?"

"Something loud," Anna replied. "And preferably with a lot of pretty lights."

Waldo rummaged in his backpack, producing a small, innocuous-looking device. "How about a localized EMP coupled with a pyrotechnic display? It'll fry their comms and give them one hell of a fireworks show."

Anna nodded. "Do it."

As Dastan's truck roared up the beach access road, Waldo leaned out the window. With practiced ease, he armed the device and hurled it toward their abandoned speedboat.

For a moment, nothing happened. Then the night exploded into chaos.

Chapter 10

A blinding flash of light erupted from the boat, followed by a thunderous boom that shook the truck. The speedboat disintegrated in a spectacular shower of sparks and flame, lighting up the beach like daylight.

In the rearview mirror, Anna watched the border patrol vehicle skid to a halt, its headlights flickering and dying as the EMP wave washed over it. The guards tumbled out, weapons drawn, staring in bewilderment at the pyrotechnic display on the beach.

"Nice work," she said to Waldo, allowing herself a small smile.

The hacker beamed, clearly pleased with himself. "I aim to please. Though I think I might have overdone it a bit on the boom factor."

Dastan's grip was tight on the steering wheel as he navigated the winding coastal road. "That'll buy us some time, but not much. We need to get off this road and onto the back routes."

Casper leaned forward, his voice tense. "What's our play, Dastan?"

The fixer's eyes darted to the rearview mirror, checking for pursuit. "Ah, don't worry. Your check cleared." A grin. "Dastan pays his debts."

He veered up a dusty road, and suddenly, two more vehicles came surging by, heading in the opposite direction.

Anna tensed, but a second later, she spotted Dastan relax his grip on the steering wheel. "Friends?" she guessed.

The middle-aged man winked at her. There was a friendly quality to his gaze, but one she didn't trust. In a way, he almost reminded her of Waldo.

As Dastan's truck bumped along the rutted dirt road, the landscape began to change. The rugged coastline gave way to rolling steppes, vast grasslands stretching to the horizon. In the predawn light, Anna could make out herds of horses grazing in the distance, their silhouettes stark against the pale sky.

"Welcome to the heart of Kazakhstan," Dastan announced, his voice tinged with pride. "Land of nomads and warriors."

The road wound through low hills, dotted with yurts—traditional round tents made of felt and wood. Smoke curled from the tops of some, hinting at the lives being lived within. As they crested a rise, a sprawling village came into view, a collection of modern houses interspersed with more traditional dwellings.

Dastan guided the truck through narrow streets, nodding to a few early risers who regarded the vehicle with curious looks. He pulled up in front of a modest house on the outskirts of the village, its walls painted a cheerful blue.

"Home sweet home," he said, cutting the engine. "We'll lay low here for a few hours, get some food in you. My wife makes the best beshbarmak in all of Kazakhstan."

As they entered the house, delicious aromas wafted from the kitchen. A woman in her forties, her dark hair streaked with gray, emerged, wiping her hands on an apron. She greeted Dastan with a quick kiss before turning to the group with a warm smile.

"Welcome, welcome," she said in accented English. "I am Ainur. Please, make yourselves comfortable. The meal is almost ready."

Anna watched as Beth and Waldo sank gratefully onto cushions in the main room, while Casper engaged Dastan in quiet conversation. The interior of the house was a blend of modern convenience and traditional Kazakh decor. Colorful rugs adorned the floors, and intricate tapestries hung on the walls, depicting scenes of horsemen and epic battles.

Ainur bustled back into the kitchen, and Anna followed, drawn by both curiosity and a desire to keep an eye on their surroundings. The kitchen was small but efficient, centered around a large wood-burning stove. A pot of something savory bubbled away, filling the air with the scent of herbs and slow-cooked meat.

"Beshbarmak," Ainur explained, noticing Anna's interest. "Our national dish. It means 'five fingers' because traditionally it is eaten with the hands." She lifted the lid, revealing tender chunks of lamb mixed with flat noodles and onions. "The meat is horse or mutton, boiled for hours until it falls off the bone."

As Ainur worked, she showed Anna the traditional bread, baursak—small, puffy fried dough balls that she said were essential for any Kazakh celebration.

Despite her fascination with Ainur's culinary know-how, Anna couldn't help but notice the hushed conversation taking place in the adjacent room. Casper and Dastan stood close together, their voices low and urgent. Anna strained to catch snippets of their discussion, but the sizzle of frying baursak and Ainur's steady stream of commentary made it difficult to discern more than a few words.

She observed their body language, though, noting the tension in Casper's shoulders and the way Dastan's eyes darted occasionally toward the kitchen. Whatever they were discussing, it was clear that both men were taking it seriously.

Finally, after what seemed like an eternity of whispered negotiation, Casper and Dastan shook hands firmly. The set of Casper's jaw suggested a mixture of relief and lingering concern as he made his way toward the kitchen.

"Anna," he said, his voice quiet as he approached. "We need to talk."

She nodded, excusing herself from Ainur's cooking lesson with a polite smile. Casper led her to a silent corner of the house, away from curious ears.

"The plan's a go," he began without preamble. "We leave first thing tomorrow. Dastan's arranged everything—transport, documents, even the falcons."

Anna smiled, relief washing over her. But Casper's expression remained terse, prompting her to ask, "What's the catch?"

Casper sighed, running a hand through his short-cropped hair. "The billionaire, Atayev? He knows who you are, Anna. That's why he agreed to this whole scheme in the first place. Your reputation as the Guardian Angel got us through the door."

Anna's eyes narrowed, her muscles tensing involuntarily. "How much does he know?"

"Enough to be dangerous," Casper replied grimly. "He's fascinated by you. Your exploits, your skills. He wants to meet you in person before we cross the border."

Anna's jaw clenched. "I don't like this, Casper. We're exposing ourselves unnecessarily."

"I know," Casper replied, his voice low and urgent. "But we don't have a choice. Atayev's influence is the only thing that'll get us into Turkmenistan without raising alarms. And after that stunt on the beach, we need all the help we can get."

Anna closed her eyes for a moment, weighing their options. When she opened them again, her gaze was steeled with determination. "Fine. But I set the terms of the meeting. And I want to know everything about this Atayev. Every detail, no matter how small."

Casper shifted, relief evident in his posture. "Deal. Dastan's got a file on him. I'll brief you after we eat."

As if on cue, Ainur's voice rang out from the kitchen, calling everyone to the table. The rich aroma of the beshbarmak filled the house, momentarily distracting from the tension of their situation.

The meal passed in a blur of flavors and conversation. Anna found herself seated next to a sharp-eyed woman named Leyla who seemed to be evaluating every word and gesture. Across the table, Beth chatted animatedly with Ainur, while Waldo peppered Dastan with questions about Turkmen technology and infrastructure.

As the plates were cleared away, Dastan clapped his hands together. "Now, my friends, we retire. Tomorrow is going to be an early morning."

As night fell, Dastan led them to a small guesthouse adjacent to the main building. The structure was simple but well-maintained, its wooden walls weathered by years of harsh winds. Inside, the air was heavy with the scent of dried herbs and wool.

Anna's trained eyes swept the room, cataloging potential exits and vantage points. Two narrow windows faced the courtyard, their glass clouded with age. A sturdy door at the back opened onto a small garden, overgrown with hardy native plants. The furniture was sparse but functional—two narrow beds with colorful quilts, a rough-hewn table, and a pair of straight-backed chairs.

The men were shown to one partition, and the two sisters to the other.

As the door shut behind them, Beth sighed heavily. Anna didn't, already scanning the room for hidden surveillance—one could never be too careful. But after a few seconds, she decided the furnishings were clean. Beth moved to the far bed, her shoulders slumped with exhaustion. She set her bag down with a soft thump, the sound seeming to echo in the room. Anna noticed her sister's hands trembling slightly as she unpacked a few essentials from her overstuffed duffel. The chocolate trail mix emerged first.

Beth lay down, and the two sisters retreated into a companionable silence.

Several minutes after Anna settled onto her own bed, the ancient springs creaking under her weight, she heard a muffled sound from Beth's side of the room. At first, she thought it might be the wind outside, whistling through some unseen crack. But then it came again—a choked, strangled noise that Anna recognized all too well.

Beth was crying.

Anna lay still, uncertain. Emotions had never been her strong suit. In the field, she knew exactly how to react to any situation—threat assessment, tactical response, extraction protocols. But this?

She could hear Beth trying to stifle her sobs, probably thinking Anna was asleep. Each muffled gasp seemed to hang in the air between them, a reminder of the pain and fear Beth had been carrying since this ordeal began.

For a long moment, Anna remained motionless, torn between her instinct to comfort her sister and her lifelong habit of emotional distance. The sound of Beth's weeping tugged at something deep within her.

Finally, decision made, Anna rose silently from her bed. Her bare feet made no sound on the rough wooden floor as she crossed the small room. Without a word, she lay down next to Beth, close enough that their shoulders touched.

Beth stiffened for a moment, then seemed to collapse into herself, her body wracked with silent sobs. Anna hesitated, then slowly, awkwardly, put an arm around her sister's shaking shoulders.

They remained like that, neither speaking. The moon rose outside, casting long shadows through the clouded windows. In the distance, a dog barked, the sound carrying clearly across the sleeping village.

Anna said nothing, but she stayed, her arm a steady presence around Beth's shoulders. As the night wore on, Beth's sobs gradually subsided, replaced by the slow, even breathing of exhausted sleep.

Only then did Anna allow herself to close her eyes, her back rigid against the headboard, ever vigilant even in rest.

Tomorrow morning, they'd meet a billionaire who'd help smuggle them into a closed nation.

But the billionaire knew Anna's name. Which meant, as it almost always did, that he *wanted* something.

Only time would tell if she could pay the asking price.

Chapter 11

The next morning, their drive to the private estate passed in silence. Beth sat closely against Anna. Neither sister had spoken about the night. Neither had needed to.

A part of Anna envied Beth.

She wondered what it would be like to release emotions in front of others... To allow someone else *into* the pain. To share it?

She found the envy growing. And so she practiced what she did best. She compartmentalized the feeling, released a slow breath, and extended her senses to observe the passing country out the window. Focus on the external. Plan. Execute.

There, ahead, she spotted the billionaire's estate. Not that it could have been mistaken for anything else.

The estate loomed before them, a sprawling compound that seemed to defy the harsh landscape surrounding it. High walls of polished stone encircled the property, topped with discreet but undoubtedly high-tech security measures. As they approached the main gate, Anna noticed cameras swiveling to track their vehicle's movement.

The contrast between the opulent estate and the surrounding grassland was jarring. While the endless grasslands stretched to the horizon, dotted with the occasional yurt or humble farmstead, Atayev's compound rose like a mirage of wealth and excess.

The main building was a fusion of modern architecture and traditional Kazakh design. Its sleek lines and floor-to-ceiling windows were softened by intricate mosaics and carved wooden panels reminiscent of ancient nomadic art. A golden dome, like a warrior's helmet, crowned the central structure, gleaming in the morning sun.

The gates swung open, revealing a long driveway lined with perfectly manicured trees.

As they passed through the gates, Anna took in every detail. Fountains burbled merrily, their water a precious commodity in this arid region. Peacocks strutted across the grounds, their iridescent feathers a splash of improbable color against the muted tones of the wild grasses beyond.

As their pickup pulled to a stop in front of the mansion with the golden dome, Anna's eyes darted from point to point. She noted the positioning of security cameras, the subtle bulges in the jackets of staff members that betrayed concealed weapons, the way the landscaping, while beautiful, offered clear lines of sight for any defenders.

A greeter in a maroon jacket and white gloves hailed them down. The man looked to be in his mid-thirties, with features that would've been quite handsome if not for the scar roping through his lips and up the left side of his cheek.

One white glove halted them and the other gestured at them to emerge. Three men with submachine guns stood to attention behind the greeter, each of the soldiers wearing blue-purple berets, the same color as some of the peacock feathers.

The guards moved with military precision, their steps perfectly in sync as they patrolled the perimeter. Their movements were too coordinated, too rehearsed for simple private security. Anna's suspicions deepened—these men had training beyond what a typical wealthy man's protection detail would require.

Near one of the compound's walls, a group of children played basketball. The incongruity of their carefree laughter against the backdrop of armed guards and opulent wealth was jarring. Anna watched as a young boy made a shot, the ball arcing gracefully through the air before swishing through the net. The children's presence felt staged, a carefully orchestrated scene of normalcy in a place that was anything but normal.

A caravan of vehicles caught Anna's attention—a fleet of sleek, armored SUVs and luxury sedans lined up near a side entrance. Their polished surfaces gleamed in the sunlight, a mix of brands that spoke of extreme wealth: Bentleys, Rolls-Royces, and several models Anna recognized as custom-built for heads of state. The vehicles were clearly prepped for departure, drivers standing at attention beside their charges. She wondered if this was their ticket through the Turkmenistan border.

Despite the flurry of activity—staff members hurrying about their tasks, security personnel scanning the grounds—there was no sign of Atayev himself. The absence of the compound's owner only heightened Anna's unease. In her experience, men like Atayev loved to make an entrance, to showcase their power and influence. His lack of immediate presence suggested either extreme caution or a flair for the dramatic.

As they were led toward the main building, Anna couldn't shake the feeling that they were walking into an elaborately constructed stage set. Every detail, from the meticulously groomed gardens to the precisely positioned guards, felt deliberate and carefully controlled. It was a display of wealth and power, yes, but also a message—one that said Atayev was a man who left nothing to chance.

The ornate front doors swung open, revealing a cavernous entryway adorned with priceless artwork and glittering chandeliers. As they stepped inside, the cool air filled with the scent of exotic flowers, Anna steeled herself for whatever game Atayev was playing.

He knew her name, and now he was making an impression.

The bigger the impression, the bigger the pockets... the bigger the ask.

This wasn't her first experience with a man used to buying what he wanted. Her gaze slipped back toward ornate twin stairs curving up on each side of the atrium. More servants lined the hall, and more guards stood at the top of the stairs.

One guard in particular stood out to Anna. Something about him caused her to pause. He didn't move like the others, with the stilted, regimented motions of people accustomed to endless drills and training. He stood relaxed, like an animal watching from under hooded eyes.

The man wore a black turtleneck and appeared to be of Eastern Asian descent. His muscles were evident, clearly built for acrobatic motion in dangerous situations. He was the sort of man who could be trusted in a firefight *and* to haul ass when needed.

Anna studied the guard, and his eyes met hers. She didn't glance away but instead held his gaze, watching him with the same intensity he watched her, like a couple of predators who'd spotted each other across familiar hunting grounds.

Suddenly, a commotion from outside broke the spell. The sound of animal groans, accompanied by shouts and the blaring of horns, drew everyone's attention to the main entrance.

The massive doors swung open once more, and a gust of wind carrying the scent of dust and animal musk swept through the atrium. Framed in the doorway was the man they'd been waiting for.

Gurbanguly Atayev, the billionaire oligarch, made his entrance astride a massive Bactrian camel. The two-humped beast, adorned with elaborate jeweled harnesses and gold-threaded tapestries, filled the doorway, its long neck swaying as it ambled forward.

Atayev himself was a picture of excess. His enormous frame, swathed in a tailored suit of shimmering gold fabric, spilled over the camel's humps. A thick walrus mustache adorned his jowly face, each end waxed and curled with painstaking precision.

Atop his head sat a fur hat of impressive proportions, festooned with peacock feathers and what appeared to be actual gems.

As the camel lumbered into the atrium, its padded feet soft on the marble floor, Atayev's booming laugh filled the space. "Welcome, welcome!" he called out, his voice carrying the practiced warmth of a man used to commanding rooms. "My dear friends, what an honor to have you in my humble home!"

With surprising agility for a man of his size, Atayev dismounted the camel, aided by two attendants who seemed to materialize from thin air. As his feet touched the ground, he spread his arms wide, beaming at Anna and her companions.

"Ah, but where are my manners?" he exclaimed, striding forward. His gait was surprisingly light for such a large man, as he almost bounced on the balls of his feet. "I am Gurbanguly Atayev, your host and, I hope, your new friend!"

He approached Anna first, his small eyes twinkling with undisguised fascination. "And you must be the famous Anna Gabriel," he said, taking her hand in both of his meaty paws. "The Guardian Angel herself! My dear, the stories I've heard... but they do not do justice to your beauty and grace!"

Anna tensed at the contact but maintained her composure, offering a polite nod in return. Atayev, seemingly oblivious to her discomfort, continued his effusive greeting.

"And this vision of loveliness must be your sister, Beth," he said, turning to plant a kiss on Beth's hand. "My dear, you are as radiant as the sunrise!"

Beth managed a weak smile, clearly overwhelmed by Atayev's exuberant personality. As the billionaire carried on to greet Casper and Waldo with equal enthusiasm, Anna noticed movement from the top of the stairs.

The Asian guard in the black turtleneck descended, his strides silent and purposeful. Unlike the other security personnel, who remained at rigid attention, this man moved with the relaxed confidence of a wolf. His dark eyes never left Anna as he approached, coming to stand just behind and to the right of Atayev.

His stance was perfectly balanced, weight distributed evenly, ready to move in any direction at a moment's notice.

Atayev, still chattering away, gestured expansively. "And, of course, you've noticed my shadow! This is... Well, I'm not entirely sure what his name is, to be honest. He doesn't speak much. Or at all, really." The billionaire chuckled, the sound grating. "But he's the best at what he does, aren't you, my friend? We call him Beta."

Beta's expression remained impassive, but his eyes flickered briefly to Atayev before returning to Anna.

As Atayev continued his boisterous introductions, Beta remained a silent, watchful presence. His dark eyes scanned the group. Anna noticed the almost imperceptible tightening of his muscles as his gaze fell on Waldo, who was fidgeting nervously with the strap of his backpack.

In that moment, as if choreographed by some unseen force, several things happened at once.

A peacock, startled by the camel's presence in the atrium, let out a piercing shriek from somewhere in the gardens. The unexpected noise caused Waldo to jump, his hand instinctively reaching for his bag. At the same instant, one of Atayev's attendants stumbled, a tray of crystal glasses slipping from his grasp.

Beta moved with preternatural speed. In the split second before the glasses shattered on the marble floor, he had closed the distance to Waldo, his hand a blur as it intercepted Waldo's reaching arm. With a twist so subtle it was almost invisible, Beta redirected Waldo's momentum, spinning him away from his bag and using the hacker's own motion to propel him behind Beta's body.

Simultaneously, Beta's other hand shot out, catching the falling tray mere inches from the ground. The glasses, which had begun to topple, settled back into place with barely a clink. In the same moment, Beta righted the tray, steadied the startled attendant, and handed the man back his tray.

All of this occurred in the space of a heartbeat. By the time the echoes of the peacock's cry had faded, Beta was back in his position behind Atayev, his posture tranquil, as if nothing had happened.

Waldo blinked, looking bewildered, as if unsure how he had suddenly ended up three feet from where he had been standing. The attendant, clutching the tray of unbroken glasses, let out a shaky breath.

Atayev, who had paused mid-sentence at the commotion, let out a booming laugh. "Ah, you see? Did I not tell you he was the best? My friend, your reflexes are sharper than ever!"

"I... er... Can I have my bag?" Waldo asked.

Atayev waved a hand. "Give the man his bag, Beta. It's fine. These are friends."

The guard looked reluctant. He eyed Waldo suspiciously, but in the end, he returned the bag.

"Now then," Atayev continued, clapping his hands together. The sound echoed through the atrium like a gunshot, causing several of the more jumpy guards to twitch. "Let's not stand on ceremony! Come, come, we have much to discuss, and time is of the essence!"

He began to lead them deeper into the mansion, Beta falling into step beside him. As they walked, Anna couldn't help but notice how the other staff and security personnel gave the personal bodyguard a wide berth. Even Atayev, for all his bluster and physical presence, seemed to unconsciously angle his body away from his silent shadow.

They passed through a series of increasingly grand rooms, each more lavishly decorated than the last. Costly artwork adorned the walls—Anna recognized pieces that should have been in museums, not a private residence. Exotic animal pelts covered the floors, and the air was permeated with the scent of expensive cigars and aged leather.

All the while, Atayev kept up a steady stream of chatter, pointing out various treasures and telling outlandish stories of their acquisition. But Anna's attention remained fixed on the silent guard. He moved with them, always present.

Threat located. Assessed. Two egress. Down a hall. One egress.

Another hall.

Only exit to their rear. She frowned. Four bodyguards now stood in the doorway.

They were being led into a private chamber with no escape.

"And *this*!" Atayev suddenly declared, spreading his arms as if to embrace an ostentatious wall covered in gold and sparkling stones, "This is my treasure room." He smacked his hands together, rubbing them in excitement and releasing a giddy laugh.

He turned to his captive audience.

"Just *wait*... You won't *believe* what I have in here."

"What?" Waldo asked, looking both excited and hungry.

"Oh, my dear friend... The sort of thing *wars* have been fought over. And... the reason we're going to Turkmenistan, together. Now come... See for yourselves."

He spread his arms in a dramatic flourish. Two servants on each side of the doors inserted keys into nearly invisible key holes.

Chapter 12

Anna studied the doors to the treasure room. Intricate carvings adorned their surface, depicting scenes of ancient battles and mythical beasts. But beneath the artistry, her trained eye detected the telltale signs of reinforced steel and complex locking mechanisms. These were not mere decorative doors, but a serious security measure.

With a soft hiss of hydraulics, the massive doors swung open, revealing a room that seemed to glow from within. Anna blinked, momentarily dazzled by the sheer wealth on display.

The treasure room was a circular chamber, its walls lined with glass cases and velvet-draped pedestals. Each display held artifacts of staggering value—golden statues encrusted with jewels, ancient scrolls preserved in climate-controlled cases, weapons that looked as if they had been forged in the dawn of civilization.

But it was the center of the room that drew everyone's attention. On a raised dais, bathed in carefully directed spotlights, stood a glass case containing a single object.

It was a falcon. Or rather, a statue of a falcon, about the size of a large house cat. The bird was captured mid-strike, its wings swept back, talons extended. Every feather was rendered in careful detail, as if a living falcon had been transformed into solid gold in an instant.

Atayev strode forward, his face beaming with pride. "Behold," he said, his voice uncharacteristically reverent, "the Golden Falcon of Nisa. A treasure beyond price, lost for centuries until it found its way to me."

Anna's eyes narrowed as she studied the artifact. Fancy things cast in gold always complicated matters. Money, power, sex... They often exaggerated human behavior.

Casper let out a low whistle. "That's... impressive," he said, clearly trying to sound nonchalant. "I assume this is related to our cover as falconers?"

Atayev's eyes glittered with excitement. "Oh, my friend, it is so much more than that. This falcon is our key to unlocking secrets that have been buried for millennia. Secrets that certain parties in Turkmenistan would kill to possess."

He turned to Anna, his expression suddenly serious. "That is why I needed you, Guardian Angel. Your skills, your reputation—they are essential for what comes next."

Anna felt a chill run down her spine. She had known this wasn't a simple smuggling operation, but the gravity of what Atayev was implying...

"What exactly are you proposing?" she asked, her voice carefully neutral.

Atayev's grin widened, revealing teeth capped in gold. "My dear, we are going to steal the falcon's mate. And in doing so, we will uncover a secret that will reshape the balance of power in Central Asia."

As Atayev spoke, Anna noticed Beta tensing almost imperceptibly.

"You see, this falcon is only half of a matched set. Its counterpart, the Silver Falcon, is believed to be hidden somewhere in the ancient ruins of Nisa, just outside of Ashgabat."

He began to pace, his excitement palpable. "Legend has it that when the two falcons are brought together, they reveal the location of an even greater treasure—one that could tip the scales of power in this region for generations to come."

Anna's mind raced, processing the implications. A treasure hunt in one of the world's most closed-off countries, with potential geopolitical consequences. This was far beyond what she had signed up for.

"And what does this have to do with us or our arms dealer holed up in Turkmenistan?" she asked, her voice sharp.

Atayev's smile faltered slightly. "Ah yes, your original mission. I assure you, it is all connected. The man you seek, this 'Albino'—he is deeply involved in this affair. Find the falcon, and you will find him. See—he's the one who currently *has* it."

Anna's eyes narrowed at Atayev's words. The pieces were starting to fall into place, but she didn't like the picture they were forming.

"So let me get this straight," she said. "You want us to enter Turkmenistan under the guise of falconers, locate and steal an ancient artifact of immense value, all while tracking down an international arms dealer who may or may not have information about my sister's missing family?"

Private intel, shared openly. Not her usual mode of operation. But Atayev clearly came armed with his own information, and right now, Anna was pissed. An already impossible job in a closed nation didn't need a *heist* added to it.

Atayev's grin widened, his gold teeth glinting in the bright light of the treasure room. "Precisely! You see, my dear, this is why I needed someone of your particular talents. It's a delicate operation, one that requires both finesse and... shall we say, a certain moral flexibility."

Anna felt Beth stiffen beside her. She could practically feel the waves of anxiety radiating from her sister. Casper remained stoic, but Anna noticed the slight tightening around his eyes. Waldo, for his part, looked equal parts terrified and excited.

"And what exactly do you get out of this?" Anna pressed, her gaze never leaving Atayev's face.

The billionaire's expression sobered. "Power, my girl. Information. The kind of leverage that can reshape nations." He gestured expansively. "The falcons are more than mere trinkets. They are keys to unlocking secrets that have been buried for centuries. You see, there are rumors of natural resources scouted and then hidden. The falcons are *maps* when combined, to the locations of gold mines, oil reserves, and emerald deposits. Not small quantities, but enormous reserves. And not just in my country, but the neighboring ones too..." He beamed. "So... as you see, we need each other."

Anna tried to concentrate. This was far more complicated than she had anticipated. The stakes were higher, the dangers more acute.

She glanced at Beta, the silent guard who had remained a constant, watchful presence throughout their interaction. His face remained impassive, but Anna sensed a subtle shift in his posture. He was coiled tight, ready for action at a moment's notice.

"And if we refuse?" Anna asked, already knowing the answer.

Atayev's smile didn't falter, but a darkness crept into his eyes. " Guardian Angel, surely you understand the position you're in. You need me to get into Turkmenistan. Without my influence, your chances of crossing the border undetected are... Well, let's just say they're not good."

He stepped closer, his bulk looming over Anna.

She stood her ground, meeting his gaze without flinching. The air between them crackled with tension.

"Let me be clear," Anna said, her voice low and dangerous. "We're not thieves for hire. Our mission is to find the Albino and get information about my sister's family. That's it."

Atayev's smile didn't reach his eyes. "Oh, you misunderstand. This isn't a request. It's the price of my assistance." He spread his hands in a gesture of mock helplessness. "After all, one good turn deserves another, yes?"

Anna was acutely aware of Beta's presence behind Atayev and the guards positioned at the door. The room suddenly felt much smaller, more confined.

"And if we still refuse?" Casper asked, his voice tight with barely contained anger.

Atayev's expression hardened. "Then I'm afraid our business is concluded. And I must warn you, the Turkmen authorities are quite... enthusiastic in their treatment of suspected spies." He shrugged, as if discussing the weather. "It would be such a shame for your mission to end before it even began."

Beth stepped forward, her face pale but determined. "We'll do it," she said quickly, before Anna could respond. "We'll help you get the Silver Falcon."

Anna turned to her sister, surprise and frustration warring on her face. "Beth, you don't understand what you're agreeing to—"

"I understand perfectly." Beth cut her off, her voice surprisingly steady. "This is our only chance to find my husband... my... my *children*. Whatever it takes, I'll do it."

Atayev clapped his hands together, his jovial demeanor returning instantly. "Excellent! I knew we could come to an arrangement." He turned to Anna, his eyes glittering with triumph. "You see, Guardian Angel? Sometimes it pays to be flexible."

Anna's jaw clenched, but she remained silent. She could feel the trap closing around them, options dwindling with each passing moment.

She shared a look with Casper. He shrugged back, placing the ball firmly in her court.

It was up to her, and they both knew it. She released a slow exhale. In the SEALs, they had a term for something like this: FUBAR.

The situation had spiraled far beyond their original mission parameters. They were now caught between an unscrupulous billionaire, a closed authoritarian nation, and an international arms dealer—with the added complication of a treasure hunt thrown in for good measure.

But Anna had been in tight spots before. She'd navigated war zones, outsmarted terrorists, and walked away from operations that should have ended in certain death. This was just another problem to solve, another mission to complete.

Her mind weighed the risks. Atayev held the cards right now, but every game had its weaknesses. She just needed to find the right pressure point.

"We'll do it," Anna agreed, her voice professional. "But we do this our way. No surprises, no last-minute changes. You give us everything you have on the Silver Falcon, the Albino, and the security we'll be facing. And we maintain complete operational control once we're in Turkmenistan."

Atayev tried to speak, but Anna wasn't finished. "One more thing," she added, her gaze boring into the man before her. "When this is over, you use your influence to ensure Beth's family is safely extracted, regardless of whether we succeed in acquiring the falcon. That's nonnegotiable."

For a moment, tension filled the room. Then Atayev laughed. "My dear Guardian Angel, you drive a hard bargain! But I like your spirit. Very well, I agree to your terms."

He snapped his fingers, and Beta stepped forward, producing a thick file from seemingly nowhere. "This contains everything we know about the Silver Falcon, its possible location, and the players involved," Atayev explained. "Study it well. You leave for Turkmenistan at dawn."

As Beta handed over the file, his eyes met Anna's. For the briefest moment, she saw something flicker in those dark depths—a warning, perhaps? Or was it a threat? Before she could decipher it, his impassive mask slid back into place.

Atayev gestured toward the door. "Now, my friends, let us feast! We have much to celebrate, and little time before your grand adventure begins!"

As they were led from the treasure room, Anna felt the weight of responsibility settle heavily on her shoulders. She'd faced impossible odds before, but this... this was something else entirely.

Beth squeezed her hand, a gesture of gratitude and support. Anna squeezed back, hoping her sister couldn't feel the slight tremor in her fingers.

Whatever came next, one thing was certain: their mission had just become far more dangerous than any of them had anticipated. And in the shadowy world of international espionage and ancient treasures, danger often came with a body count.

Chapter 13

The previous night's feast felt heavy in Anna's stomach, though she'd tried to eat light. Now, as their row of flashy vehicles drew near the checkpoint, she found herself jumpy. The checkpoint on the Kazakhstan–Turkmenistan border reminded her of similar crossings she'd encountered in other closed nations—a mix of imposing architecture and barely concealed menace.

Concrete barriers funneled traffic into narrow lanes, forcing vehicles to slow to a crawl. Watchtowers loomed overhead, their darkened windows concealing watchful eyes and ready weapons. Heavily armed guards patrolled the area, their faces set in masks of grim determination.

Anna sat in the back of a gleaming black SUV, wedged between Beth and Waldo. Casper rode shotgun, his posture tense as he surveyed the approaching checkpoint. In the driver's seat, one of Atayev's men guided the vehicle.

As they inched closer to the border crossing, Anna ran through their cover story one last time in her head. They were part of Atayev's falconry team, bringing prized birds for an exhibition in Ashgabat. The paperwork was impeccable, the bribes had been paid, and Atayev's influence was supposed to smooth their way.

But Anna knew better than to rely on promises and paperwork. Her hand unconsciously drifted to the small of her back, where a slim ceramic blade was concealed. It wasn't much, but it was better than nothing if things went sideways. They hadn't been able to risk keeping their weapons on them. Most of their gear was smuggled under the hay in the van holding the birds.

The SUV came to a stop at the first checkpoint. A stern-faced guard approached, his hand resting casually on the butt of his holstered pistol.

He demanded something in Turkmen.

Their driver handed over a stack of documents. The guard flipped through them with practiced efficiency, his eyes narrowing as he scrutinized each photo.

Anna held her breath, keeping her expression unreadable. Next to her, she could feel Beth trembling slightly. She reached out and squeezed her sister's hand.

The guard's gaze lingered on Anna's passport photo, his eyes flicking between the image and her face. For a heart-stopping moment, she thought he was going to raise an alarm. But then he grunted and handed the passports back to the driver.

He said something else Anna couldn't understand and then waved them forward.

As they pulled away from the first checkpoint, Anna allowed herself a small sigh of relief. But she knew they weren't in the clear yet. Secondary inspection could be even more thorough, and there were still too many ways this could go wrong.

As she stared through the windshield, she suddenly drew in a sharp breath.

Casper, sitting on her other side, noticed her attention. "What is it?" he whispered.

She stared, and then she released a slow exhale. "Kovac," she said simply.

Casper frowned and then noticed where she was looking.

There, standing by the guards at the second checkpoint, was a familiar face. The last time she'd seen him had been at night during the raid on their yacht. But clearly, the ex-Spetsnaz psycho had recovered from his swim in the Caspian Sea. And by the looks of things, he was in an argument with two of the guards, waving his hands, standing next to a stalled vehicle.

It just so happened, Kovac was in the same line as their over-the-top procession of expensive vehicles.

Multiple sets of eyes were already glued on the Rolls Royces and the gleaming SUVs in their convoy. Anna knew that if Kovac spotted them, their entire operation could be blown before it even began.

She leaned forward, speaking in a low, urgent tone to their driver. "We need to switch lanes. Now."

The driver glanced back, confusion evident on his face. "But Atayev said—"

"I don't care what Atayev said," Anna interrupted. "Do it. Unless you want this whole thing to fall apart before we even cross the border."

Something in her tone must have convinced him. With a nod, he began maneuvering their SUV into the adjacent lane, drawing annoyed honks from other vehicles.

Casper turned to Anna, his voice barely above a whisper. "What's the play here?"

"We avoid Kovac at all costs," she replied, her eyes never leaving the scene ahead. "If he recognizes us, this whole operation is blown. And I doubt the Turkmen border guards will be sympathetic to our story."

As their vehicle inched forward in the new lane, Anna watched Kovac out of the corner of her eye. He was still engaged in what appeared to be a heated discussion with the border guards, gesticulating wildly. His face was flushed with anger, a vein throbbing visibly in his forehead.

For a moment, Anna thought they might slip by unnoticed. But then, as if sensing her gaze, Kovac's head snapped around. His eyes scanned the line of vehicles, narrowing as they fell on their SUV.

The windows were tinted. There was no reason he should know who sat behind the darkened glass, yet he turned to look.

Perhaps it was simply due to the spectacle of the convoy itself.

Anna held her breath as their SUV crawled forward, Kovac's piercing gaze still fixed on their tinted windows. She could almost feel the weight of his suspicion, like a physical presence pressing against the glass. There was no way he could see through the dark tint, she reassured herself.

But if he was here, then he was cleverer than he'd been back on the boat.

And the way he was arguing with the guards—it almost seemed as if he felt he had some sort of authority they needed to acknowledge but was being caught up in the red tape of some uninformed soul lower down the totem pole. She shivered, feeling certain that this wasn't the last they'd seen of the Russian.

At last their vehicle train moved on, leaving Kovac behind them.

As they approached the second checkpoint, a new drama unfolded. Their driver, a stocky man with a neatly trimmed beard, leaned out of the window to hand over another stack of documents. The guard, a young man with a face prematurely lined by the harsh desert sun, began flipping through the papers with exaggerated slowness.

His eyes widened as he came to a particular page, and he barked something in rapid-fire Turkmen. Anna couldn't understand the words, but the tone was unmistakable—a mix of surprise and barely concealed greed.

The driver responded calmly. As he spoke, he reached into his jacket, producing a thick manila envelope. Even from her position in the back seat, Anna could see the telltale bulge of cash inside.

The guard's eyes darted left and right, checking if his colleagues were watching. Then, with a movement so smooth it was clearly practiced, he allowed the envelope to slip from the driver's hand into his own, immediately tucking it into his uniform jacket.

More words were exchanged, the guard's tone now obsequious and eager to please. He waved them forward, even offering a crisp salute as their SUV rolled past.

As they cleared the checkpoint, Anna allowed herself to relax a bit. She glanced back, watching as Kovac's figure grew smaller in the distance. He was still arguing with the guards, his face contorted with rage. Whatever strings he had tried to pull, they clearly hadn't worked as well as Atayev's influence.

The landscape began to change as they drove deeper into Turkmenistan. The barren steppe gave way to carefully irrigated fields, patches of green amid the dusty brown earth. In the distance, the glittering spires of Ashgabat rose to the sky, a city of white marble and gold leaf improbably planted in the middle of the desert.

Their driver, sensing the stress had eased, spoke up. "We are headed to the palace of Abarim Berdimaha," he announced, his accent thick but his English clear. "He is the nephew of the president, and while Turkmenistan does not officially have princes, he is as close as one can get."

Anna nodded, processing this new information. A presidential nephew—that complicated matters. The higher up their contacts were, the more dangerous the game.

As they drove further into Ashgabat, the opulence of the city became even more striking. Wide boulevards lined with perfectly trimmed trees stretched out in every direction, eerily empty despite the mid-morning hour. Gleaming skyscrapers of white marble and mirrored glass towered overhead, their spires reaching toward new heights.

Anna took in the surreal landscape. "It's like a movie set," she murmured, more to herself than the others.

Casper nodded grimly. "A very expensive movie set. Turkmenistan's been pouring billions into Ashgabat for years. All to project an image of wealth and modernity."

"But where are all the people?" Beth asked, her voice hushed with awe and unease.

"Probably told to stay off the main streets," Waldo chimed in, his face pressed against the window. "Can't have regular folks spoiling the view, right?"

As they turned onto a wide avenue, a massive golden statue came into view. It depicted a man on horseback, his arm outstretched toward the horizon.

Their driver noticed their interest. "That is our great leader," he explained, pride evident in his voice. "He guides our nation to prosperity and enlightenment."

Anna exchanged a look with Casper, both of them well aware of the realities behind Turkmenistan's facade of progress. But they kept their thoughts to themselves. In a place like this, even the walls could have ears.

The convoy of vehicles finally turned off the main road, approaching an ornate gate flanked by armed guards. Beyond the gate, a palace lay at the edge of landscaped grounds—a sprawling complex of domes, arches, and gleaming white walls.

As they pulled up to the entrance, Anna took a deep breath, centering herself. Whatever came next, she knew they were now deep in the heart of one of the world's most secretive and oppressive regimes. One false move could spell disaster not just for their mission, but for their lives.

The doors of their SUV opened, and they stepped out into the bright Turkmen sun. A group of men in immaculate suits approached, led by a young man with sharp features and an easy smile that didn't quite reach his eyes.

"Welcome, honored guests," he said, his English crisp. "I am Abarim Berdimaha. My uncle, the president, sends his warmest regards and looks forward to your falconry exhibition."

As Anna shook his hand, she felt the familiar pull of eyes on her. Glancing up, she caught sight of a figure watching from a high window of the palace. Even at this distance, she could make out the unmistakable silhouette of Beta, Atayev's silent bodyguard. He'd clearly arrived ahead of them. Perhaps to secure the premises, or perhaps for more clandestine reasons.

Anna reminded herself why they were here. If their security broker, Byers' intel was correct, then the Albino was holed up somewhere here.

It would be up to Anna to find a way out of the palace, into the city streets without being detected, in order to locate the Albino. She doubted the arms dealer would be easy to find. And if she *did* find him, he'd have more security than Kovac's little boarding party she'd dispatched.

Still. The first step of the process was now complete.

The self-styled prince swept an arm toward the palace, calling out, "Follow me!"

It was only then that Anna frowned.

He was speaking in English. And yet their cover was that of Russian bird trainers. So why the English? Perhaps he didn't know Russian?

Or perhaps he knew far, far more than she would've liked.

Another troubling thing caught her attention. As they followed Abarim into the palace, Anna noticed the young prince's gaze repeatedly drifting toward Beth.

The grandiose interior of the palace assaulted their senses—gleaming marble floors, intricate tapestries, and gold leaf seemingly covered every surface. Abarim led them through a series of increasingly lavish rooms, all eerily devoid of other people.

"And this," Abarim announced, gesturing grandly, "is our falconry chamber."

The room was circular, its domed ceiling painted with detailed scenes of falcons in flight. Perches of varying heights dotted the space, and large windows offered sweeping views of the grounds.

As the others moved to inspect the room, Abarim sidled closer to Beth. "Tell me," he purred, his voice low and intimate, "have you ever handled such magnificent creatures before?"

Beth stammered a response, clearly flustered by his proximity. Abarim placed a hand on the small of her back, guiding her toward one of the perches. His touch lingered longer than necessary, fingers splaying possessively.

"Perhaps I could give you a private lesson," he murmured, leaning in close. His other hand came to rest on Beth's arm.

Beth stiffened, clearly uncomfortable with the prince's forwardness. Anna's jaw clenched. Briefly, she forgot the army of private security, and she moved toward the prince, intent on breaking his arm. Casper caught her, though, and sidled between Beth and the prince.

In English, faking an accent, Casper said, "Why don't we discuss business, hmm?"

The prince frowned at the interruption but allowed Casper to redirect his attention. Anna wondered if the man knew how close he'd been to starting an international incident.

She took Beth aside, whispering, "Stay next to me."

Beth's head bobbed a single time.

All the while, as the tour continued and Anna glanced around the ostentatious falconry room, she found her thoughts racing. She had to keep Beth safe. Had to find the Albino. And had to do it all without pissing off a hostile regime.

She had her work cut out for her. But tonight... once they were settled in their quarters and briefed on the upcoming falconry event, then she'd have a chance to make her move.

Chapter 14

Midnight descended on Ashgabat, muffling the shining white marble and gold leaf under a blanket of darkness. Kovac stood in the shadows of an abandoned construction site, the skeletal frame of an unfinished high-rise looming above him. Despite the warm night air, he wore a heavy jacket, its bulk concealing the arsenal strapped to his body.

He hummed softly under his breath, frowning as he tried new lyrics for his own composition.

The words weren't flowing tonight, though. His muse hid from the streets the same as the nation's population.

The city's emptiness took on an eerie quality in the dark. The wide boulevards stretched out like runways, devoid of traffic or pedestrians. In the distance, the gilded domes of government buildings glinted faintly under the starlight.

Kovac's eyes, sharp despite the darkness, scanned his surroundings. His fingers twitched, longing for a cigarette, but he resisted the urge. No unnecessary movements, no telltale glows. Not here, not now.

A faint scraping sound caught his attention. Kovac tensed, his hand moving toward the pistol concealed at his hip. A figure emerged from behind a stack of rusting I-beams, striding forward with the cautious grace of a predator in unfamiliar territory.

"Dmitri," Kovac called softly.

The figure froze, then slowly turned toward Kovac's position. "Kovalev? Is that you, you crazy bastard?"

Dmitri stepped into a patch of dim moonlight, and Kovac got his first good look at his old contact. The years had not been kind. Dmitri's face was more lined, his hair grayer, and his once-muscular frame had softened with age and drink. But his eyes were as piercing as ever, darting constantly, taking in every detail of their surroundings.

Kovac noticed the bulge of body armor beneath Dmitri's shirt, the outline of at least two pistols, and the unmistakable shape of a compact submachine gun slung under his arm. Dmitri had come prepared for war.

"You're a hard man to find these days," Dmitri said, his voice gruff. He made no move to come closer, keeping a careful distance between them. "Word is you've gone rogue. Pissed off some very powerful people."

Kovac shrugged, a barely perceptible movement in the darkness. "You know how it is, Dmitri. Sometimes the job takes unexpected turns."

Dmitri's laugh was harsh, devoid of humor. "Unexpected turns? That's what you call leaving a trail of bodies across three countries? Shit, Kovalev, what the hell happened to you?"

For a moment, Kovac considered telling him. About the woman who had bested him, humiliated him.

But no. No, he'd come to Dmitri for a very specific reason.

No one else in this godforsaken country could get their hands on what he needed.

But he knew Dmitri. The prices were always high. Especially for Russians.

He also knew how paranoid the man was.

"Where's the rest of the crew?" Kovac asked, picking absentmindedly at a fingernail.

"Oh, they're watching," said the man, flashing a gap-toothed smile.

Kovac nodded, scanning the surrounding area with newfound intensity. He picked out at least three potential sniper positions in the unfinished buildings nearby. Dmitri hadn't come alone.

"Smart," Kovac said. "You always were cautious."

Dmitri's eyes narrowed. "Cut the small talk. What do you want?"

Kovac took a deep breath, steeling himself. This was the moment of truth. "I need something... special. Something that can take down a particular target."

Dmitri raised an eyebrow. "And what might that be?"

"A Guardian Angel," Kovac said, his voice barely a whisper.

Dmitri's eyes widened in recognition. "Hell, man. You're going after her? The one they call the angel of death?"

Kovac nodded grimly. "She humiliated me, Dmitri. Made me look like an amateur. I can't let that stand."

Dmitri let out a low whistle. "You're crazier than I thought. But..." he paused, a glint of greed entering his voice, "I might have something that could help. It won't come cheap, though."

"Name your price," Kovac said, his voice hard.

Dmitri named a figure that made even Kovac wince. But he nodded. "Done."

"Follow me," Dmitri said, turning to lead Kovac deeper into the abandoned construction site.

They walked through a maze of half-finished structures, their footsteps echoing in the haunting stillness. The smell of concrete dust and rusting metal hung in the air. As they descended into the bowels of the construction site, the darkness thickened, broken only by the occasional flicker of Dmitri's flashlight.

Finally, they reached what appeared to be an abandoned underground parking garage. Dmitri approached a nondescript concrete wall, running his hand along its surface until he found what he was looking for. With a soft click, a hidden panel slid open, revealing a state-of-the-art biometric scanner.

"New security measures," Dmitri muttered, pressing his palm against the cool surface. "Can't be too careful these days."

The scanner hummed to life, a blue light sweeping over Dmitri's hand. After a moment, a series of heavy locks disengaged, and a section of the wall swung inward, revealing a hidden chamber beyond.

Kovac's eyes widened as they stepped inside. The room was a stark contrast to the decrepit construction site above. Shiny metal shelves lined the walls, each holding an array of weaponry that would make most military commanders weep with envy.

Six security officers all lined the walls, each of them eyeing Kovac suspiciously. His reputation preceded him. Not a single safety was on. But Kovac's gaze was drawn to a case at the far end of the room.

Dmitri noticed his interest and grinned. "Ah, you have good taste, my friend. That's what you came for, isn't it?"

He approached the case, entering a complex code into a keypad. With a hiss of escaping air, the case opened, revealing its contents.

"Behold," Dmitri said, his voice tinged with reverence, "the XM2010 Enhanced Sniper Rifle. But not just any XM2010. This is a prototype. The next generation, not even in production yet."

Kovac stepped closer, his breath catching in his throat. The rifle was a work of art, its lines sleek and purposeful. The stock was made of an advanced polymer, reducing weight without sacrificing strength. The barrel was crafted from a proprietary alloy that promised unparalleled accuracy and heat dispersion.

"This beauty," Dmitri continued, "has an effective range of over 1,800 meters. The scope is military-grade, with thermal imaging and an advanced ballistic computer. It can compensate for wind speed, temperature, even the Coriolis effect."

Kovac's fingers itched to touch it, to feel the perfect balance and precision of the weapon. "And the ammunition?"

Dmitri's grin widened. "That's where things get really interesting." He pulled out a small case, opening it to reveal a set of rounds unlike anything Kovac had seen before. "These are experimental. Armor-piercing, yet they fragment on impact for maximum damage. They're guided, too. Once you fire, they can retarget up to three feet."

Kovac's eyes widened as he examined the rounds. "Guided bullets? How is that possible?"

"Micro-fins and an onboard guidance system. Once fired, they can adjust their trajectory midflight. Makes it nearly impossible to miss, even at extreme ranges."

Kovac nodded slowly. With a weapon like this, he could take out the Guardian Angel from over a mile away. She'd never see it coming.

"I'll take it," he said, his voice low and intense. "All of it."

Dmitri raised an eyebrow. "Are you sure? The price..."

"I don't care about the price," Kovac snapped. "I want her dead."

Dmitri studied him for a long moment, then shrugged. "Very well. But I warn you, Kovalev. This vendetta of yours... It's going to get you killed."

Kovac's eyes blazed with a manic intensity. "Maybe. But not before I send that bitch to hell."

As Dmitri packed up the rifle and ammunition, Kovac began thinking of a plan. He had the tool he needed now. All that remained was to find his target.

In a city as tightly controlled as Ashgabat, with every entrance and exit monitored, it was only a matter of time before the Guardian Angel showed herself. When she did, he would be ready.

Granted, there was one *other* thing.

Kovac reached for the case containing the rifle, but Dmitri's hand shot out, gripping his wrist with surprising strength.

"Not so fast," Dmitri said, his voice a warning. "Payment first."

Kovac's jaw clenched. This was the moment he'd known would be tricky. "About that," he began, choosing his words carefully. "I'm going to need the rifle on... credit."

Dmitri's eyes narrowed, his grip on Kovac's wrist tightening. "Credit? You must be joking."

"I'm good for it," Kovac insisted. "You know my reputation. Once the job is done, I'll have more than enough to cover the cost."

Dmitri released Kovac's wrist, taking a step back. His hand drifted toward the pistol at his hip. "Your reputation? Your reputation is garbage right now, Kovalev. You're a wild dog again. No backers, no support. Just a man with a grudge and a death wish. Half your team is dead from what I heard."

Kovac bristled at the intimation. Normally, if someone talked to him like that, it cost them their tongue. But he kept his cool. For now. "Think about it, Dmitri. When I take out the Guardian Angel, my stock will skyrocket. Every agency, every government will be clamoring for my services. I'll be able to name my price."

"If you survive," Dmitri countered. "And that's a very big *if*."

The guards along the walls shifted, their hands tightening on their weapons. Kovac could feel the situation slipping away from him.

"I need this, Dmitri," he said, his voice firm.

Dmitri shook his head, a mixture of pity and disgust on his face. "You've lost it, Kovalev. This obsession... It's going to be the death of you."

For a long moment, silence reigned in the underground chamber. Kovac could hear his own heart pounding in his ears, feel the desperation clawing at his insides. Everything hinged on this moment.

Finally, Dmitri spoke. "No deal," he said, his voice flat and final. "I don't do charity work, and I certainly don't arm madmen on credit."

Kovac felt the last shred of his control slipping away. His hand inched toward his concealed weapon, muscles ready for action. But before he could make a move, the guards reacted.

In an instant, six weapons were trained on him, their laser sights painting red dots across his chest and forehead. Kovac froze.

Leverage. In these moments, it was all about leverage.

And with these types? The only leverage was money.

The man who *paid* the bills of these armed men was standing across from Kovac, glaring. The six thugs aimed their triggers at him.

But it didn't matter.

Kovac's thoughts raced. The guards were well-positioned. But he hadn't survived this long by playing it safe.

In a blur of motion almost too fast for the eye to follow, Kovac exploded into action. He dropped low, his body a coiled spring of lethal intent. Before the guards could shoot, he surged forward, closing the distance to Dmitri.

The world seemed to slow around him as adrenaline flooded his system. He could see every detail with crystal clarity—the widening of Dmitri's eyes as realization dawned, the minute adjustments of the guards' aim as they struggled to track him, the faint shimmer of dust in the air, disturbed by his sudden attack.

Kovac's hand shot out, fingers wrapping around Dmitri's throat with vise-like strength. In the same moment, he spun the arms dealer around, using him as a human shield. His other hand produced a wickedly sharp combat knife, pressing it against Dmitri's jugular.

"Ne strelyayte!" Dmitri screamed in Russian, his voice strangled by Kovac's grip. "Don't shoot!"

The guards hesitated, their fingers twitching on triggers but not daring to fire. Kovac could see the uncertainty in their eyes, the fear of hitting their employer.

Dmitri's body trembled against him, the man's pulse racing beneath the blade. Kovac could smell the sour stench of fear emanating from his hostage, feel the rapid rise and fall of his chest.

"Now then," Kovac said, his voice unnervingly calm, "let's renegotiate those terms, shall we?"

Dmitri struggled against Kovac's iron grip, his feet scrabbling on the concrete floor. Beads of sweat formed on his brow, trickling down to mingle with the blood welling up where Kovac's blade pressed against his skin. The arms dealer's eyes darted frantically between his guards, silently pleading for help.

Kovac's grasp was like a steel band around Dmitri's throat, unyielding. Despite Dmitri's desperate attempts to break free, twisting and thrashing with all his might, Kovac held him effortlessly. The ex-Spetsnaz operative's breath was calm and steady, a striking contrast to Dmitri's ragged gasps.

"Tell them to lower their weapons," Kovac demanded, his voice a growl that sent shivers down Dmitri's spine.

Dmitri's face contorted with rage and fear. "Go to hell, Kovalev!" he spat, his words choked and strained. "You're dead, you hear me? Dead!"

Kovac's response was to constrict his grip, cutting off Dmitri's air supply. The knife edge bit deeper, a thin line of crimson spreading along its length. He leaned in close, his lips nearly touching Dmitri's ear, and whispered a threat so softly that only Dmitri could hear it.

All color drained from Dmitri's face, his eyes widening in abject terror.

"O-okay," Dmitri gasped, his voice shaking. "Okay, just... please..."

He raised a hand toward his guards. "L-lower your weapons," he commanded. "Do it now!"

The guards exchanged uncertain glances, clearly torn between following orders and protecting their employer.

"Now!" Dmitri screamed, hysteria edging into his voice.

Slowly, reluctantly, the guards lowered their weapons. The red dots painting Kovac's body winked out one by one, leaving the room in taut silence.

"Grab the rifle," Kovac snapped.

Dmitri's hand trembled as he reached for the rifle case, his movements fumbling and hesitant. Kovac's grip remained firm, the knife edge a constant deadly pressure against Dmitri's throat. The arms dealer's fingers struggled with the latches, nearly dropping the case before finally securing it.

"The ammunition too," Kovac hissed, his breath hot against Dmitri's ear.

Dmitri grabbed the small case containing the experimental rounds. Sweat trickled down into his eyes. He blinked rapidly, trying to clear his vision.

Kovac retreated toward the exit, dragging Dmitri with him. The guards watched helplessly, their weapons lowered but bodies on alert, ready to spring into action at the slightest opportunity.

As they neared the door, Kovac's eyes darted around the room, taking in every detail. The metal shelves of weapons, the state-of-the-art security systems, the nervous twitches of the guards' trigger fingers as they readied to raise and fire in one motion. His gaze settled on a shelf near the exit, where a row of grenades sat innocuously, their dull surfaces betraying no hint of their destructive potential.

"Place the rifle on the ground outside."

Dmitri complied, putting the ammo box on top of the sniper's case just outside the secured room.

Then, in a lightning-fast move, Kovac's free hand shot out, snatching one of the grenades. The guards' eyes widened in horror as they realized what was happening, but it was already too late.

With skillful ease, Kovac pulled the pin with his teeth, holding the safety lever down with his thumb. The soft "ping" of the pin hitting the concrete floor seemed to echo in the room.

"No!" one of the guards shouted, raising his weapon.

But Kovac was already moving. He shoved Dmitri forward, sending the arms dealer stumbling into his men. In the same motion, he slipped through the door, slamming it shut behind him.

The heavy metal door had barely closed when Kovac released the safety lever. He counted silently in his head as he sprinted down the corridor, the rifle case and ammunition clutched to his chest.

One... two... three...

The explosion rocked the underground complex, the concussive force nearly knocking Kovac off his feet. The sound was deafening, even through the thick concrete walls. Dust and debris filled the air, choking and blinding him.

But Kovac didn't slow down. He ran, his footsteps echoing in the chaos, the prize he'd come for secured in his grip. Behind him, he could hear muffled screams and the crackle of flames, but he didn't look back.

He'd gotten what he came for. The Guardian Angel's days were numbered.

Chapter 15

Anna placed the small communication device into her ear. "Casper?" she said, pressing her finger against the nearly invisible insert.

A pause, some static, and then the channel zoned in. "Copy. En route?"

Anna lowered her hand. It was the mark of an amateur to constantly touch one's ear. Giving into the discomfort immediately identified the operative *as* an operative.

Anna scanned her lavish guest quarters one last time, ensuring every detail was in place. The room was studded with riches—ornate gold filigree adorned the walls, colorful tapestries depicted ancient hunting scenes, and the plush carpet was thick enough to swallow her footsteps. A crystal chandelier cast shifting patterns across the marble floor, its light catching on the gilded edges of antique furniture.

She moved to the window, peering out at the gardens below. Topiary animals stood frozen in mid-leap, their leafy forms casting long shadows in the moonlight. Fountains burbled softly, their waters glinting like liquid silver. In the distance, she could make out the silhouettes of armed guards patrolling the perimeter.

A soft knock at the door made her jump. She relaxed as Casper's voice came through her earpiece. "Ready?"

Anna opened the door, revealing her former teammate dressed in the uniform of a palace guard. The ill-fitting clothes strained against his muscular frame, but in the dim light of the hallway, he'd pass a cursory inspection.

"Let's move," Anna whispered, slipping into the corridor. "Waldo has our gear at the third exit."

Casper grumbled, "Not all of us memorize blueprints. Lead the way."

They made their way through the labyrinthine palace, every sense on high alert. At every turn they saw rare artifacts in glass cases, exotic plants in gilded pots, even the occasional caged bird, its plumage a riot of color in the muted light.

As they descended a sweeping staircase, the distant sound of music reached their ears. Somewhere in the vast complex, a late-night party was in full swing. The faint strains of a string quartet mingled with the tinkling of crystal and muffled laughter.

"Abarim's hosting some sort of soiree," Casper murmured. "Could work to our advantage. More chaos to hide in."

They passed a series of doors, each more imposing than the last. Behind one, Anna caught a glimpse of a room filled floor to ceiling with books, their leather spines lustrous in the soft light of reading lamps. Another revealed a private cinema, its screen frozen on a paused frame of some action movie.

As they neared the ground floor, the scent of rich food wafted through the air—spices, roasted meats, and the cloying sweetness of desserts. Anna's stomach growled involuntarily, reminding her that it had been hours since she'd last eaten.

They paused at an intersection, pressing themselves against the wall as a group of laughing partygoers stumbled past, their clothing a riot of silk and jewels. Once the coast was clear, Anna and Casper slipped down a side corridor, heading toward a service entrance they'd identified earlier.

"There," Anna muttered, nodding ahead. "Waldo should be waiting back—"

She trailed off, her eyes drawn to a nearby window. She stared.

"Anna?" Casper whispered at her side.

But she didn't listen. Her eyes were fixated on where the prince was marching with four bodyguards across the garden. He was heading to the east wing, moving swiftly under the bright moonlight.

"Anna?" Casper tugged at her arm.

"I'll catch up," she mumbled. "Just... just behind you."

"What? No—we need to go *now*."

But she didn't reply.

Anna's eyes narrowed as she watched Prince Abarim and his entourage. Their purposeful stride and the late hour set off alarm bells in her mind. The prince's earlier behavior toward Beth flashed through her memory—his lingering touches, the predatory glint in his eyes. A cold knot formed in the pit of her stomach.

"He's heading toward Beth's wing," Anna said, her voice tight with concern.

Fountains dotted the landscape, their waters sparkling like liquid diamonds as they cascaded into mercurial pools. The gentle splashing mingled with the lively music from the ongoing party.

But Anna saw none of this beauty. Her eyes remained fixed on the prince and his guards as they disappeared behind a towering topiary shaped like a rearing stallion.

"Anna, we need to go," Casper urged, his voice insistent. "The window for exfiltration is closing."

She turned to him, her green eyes blazing. "I'll meet you at the motor pool."

Casper's jaw clenched, frustration evident in the set of his shoulders. "This isn't the plan. We're supposed to be finding the Albino, remember?"

Anna was already moving toward a side door that would lead her into the gardens. "I'll catch up. Just... keep Waldo safe and be ready to move when I give the signal."

"You have fifteen minutes," Casper snapped. "That's one five! You better be there. We can't wait."

Before Casper could protest further, Anna slipped through the door and into the night. The cool air hit her skin, carrying with it the heady scent of night-blooming jasmine. She moved swiftly but silently, her feet treading on the smooth gravel paths.

She paused behind a massive urn overflowing with trailing vines, her breath coming in controlled exhales.

The east wing loomed before her, its windows glowing warmly against the night sky. Balconies jutted from the upper floors, their wrought iron railings twisting into fantastical shapes. Anna's gaze zeroed in on one particular balcony—Beth's room.

A movement caught her eye. Prince Abarim and his entourage entered a side door, their footsteps hidden by the thick carpet that spilled out onto the terrace. The prince's face was flushed, his eyes glittering with barely contained excitement. He gestured animatedly to his guards, who fanned out around him like the feathers of a preening peacock.

They disappeared into the east wing. Anna didn't hesitate.

She didn't head toward the same entrance, though, but rather beelined for the balcony to Beth's room.

Anna approached the base of the east wing, her eyes scanning the facade for handholds. The building's intricate architecture—a fusion of classical and modern styles—provided many options for her ascent. Cornices, decorative pilasters, and deep-set windows created a vertical playground for someone with her skills.

She took a deep breath, centering herself. Then, with fluid grace, she began to climb.

Her fingers grabbed the rough stone of a carved gargoyle, its snarling expression a startling contrast to the elegance surrounding it. She hauled herself up, muscles straining as she sought her next hold. A series of protruding windowsills provided a zigzagging path upward, each one barely wide enough for the edge of her foot.

Anna paused at a narrow ledge, pressing her body flat against the cool stone. A guard passed on the balcony below, his flashlight beam sweeping across the grounds. She held her breath, blending with the shadows until the danger passed.

With a final burst of effort, she vaulted over the railing of Beth's balcony, landing in a silent crouch. For a moment, she remained still, listening intently for any sign that her approach had been detected. Hearing nothing but the distant music from the ongoing party, she straightened and moved to the French doors.

Anna tapped gently on the glass, a prearranged pattern that Beth would recognize. Seconds ticked by, each one feeling like an eternity. Finally, the curtain twitched aside, revealing Beth's sleep-tousled face. Her eyes widened in surprise, then recognition.

As Beth fumbled with the lock, Anna glanced over her shoulder, scanning the gardens below. The coast remained clear, but she knew their window of opportunity was rapidly closing.

Fifteen minutes to meet up at the motor pool.

But some things mattered more.

The door opened with a soft click, and Anna slipped inside, pressing a finger to her lips. Beth nodded, her expression a mixture of relief and apprehension as Anna closed the door behind them, drawing the heavy curtains to conceal their presence from prying eyes.

"What's wrong?" Beth began to whisper, but Anna gave a quick shake of her head.

She hurried toward the doors. She could hear footsteps down the hall. Swiftly, Anna dragged the weighty mahogany dresser across the plush carpet, its brass handles jingling softly as she positioned it against the door. The dresser's bulk, amplified by drawers filled with silks and linens, created a formidable barricade.

She had barely stepped back when a gentle knock sounded at the door. Beth's eyes filled with fear, her fingers clutching the bedspread so tightly her knuckles turned white. The four-poster bed, with its canopy of shimmering gold fabric, seemed to dwarf her trembling form.

The metallic scrape of a key in the lock echoed through the room. Anna gestured for Beth to remain silent. The door handle jiggled, then stilled as it met the resistance of the dresser.

"My dear Beth," Prince Abarim's voice oozed through the crack, dripping with false charm. "Why don't you open the door? I thought we might continue our... conversation from earlier."

Beth shrank back against the headboard in the dim light. Her eyes darted to Anna, silently pleading for help.

Anna remained motionless, her body coiled and ready for action. Her gaze swept the room, taking in potential weapons and escape routes. A delicate Fabergé egg perched on a nearby table, its jeweled surface glinting invitingly. A letter opener, shaped like a miniature scimitar, lay abandoned on a writing desk.

"Beth?" The prince's voice took on an edge of irritation. "I know you're awake."

The pounding on the door grew more insistent. The dresser shuddered with each impact, its legs scraping against the floor. A vase of flowers on top teetered precariously, petals scattering.

"Open this door immediately!" Abarim's voice had lost all pretense of charm, raw anger seeping through. "Do you know who I am? What I can do to you?"

The threats continued, each one more graphic than the last. Beth whimpered softly, burying her face in her hands. The moonlight filtering through the window cast shadows across her face, accentuating her terror.

Anna's jaw clenched, her eyes hardening with fury. She glanced at her watch—precious minutes ticking away. The rendezvous at the motor pool loomed.

The pounding intensified, the door frame groaning under the assault. A hairline crack appeared in one of the door's panels, spreading like a spider's web.

"This is bullshit," Anna muttered.

And then she moved.

She dragged the barricade away and swung the door wide open.

Chapter 16

Anna stood framed in the doorway, the light from the hall spotlighting her form, her posture relaxed and confident. Her white streak of hair shone like polished silver, a contrast to the darkness in her gaze.

"I'm sorry," Anna said, her voice dripping with honey-sweet venom. "I couldn't quite hear what you were saying earlier. Would you mind repeating it?"

Prince Abarim stood frozen, his mouth agape. The flush of anger that had colored his cheeks moments ago drained away, leaving him pale and stunned. His silk robe, embroidered with gold thread and studded with tiny gemstones, seemed to hang limply from his suddenly diminished frame.

Behind him, the four guards shifted uncomfortably. Their eyes darted between Anna and the prince, hands hovering near their weapons.

Anna looked over the group, taking in every detail. The guards' neat uniforms, pressed to perfection, were at odds with their nervous body language. One guard's holstered pistol glinted in the light.

The hallway stretched out behind them, its walls adorned with gilded sconces. The scent of flowers from Beth's room mingled with the metallic tang of fear emanating from the prince and his entourage.

Anna leaned casually against the doorframe, radiating calm confidence. She cocked her head slightly, a small smile playing at the corners of her mouth. Her green eyes, sharp and alert, never left the prince's face.

"Well?" she prompted, her tone light and conversational. "I'm all ears. You seemed to have so much to say just a moment ago. Something about what you could do?"

The prince swallowed hard, his Adam's apple bobbing visibly. A bead of sweat trickled down his temple, catching the light like a diamond as it fell. His fingers, adorned with heavy rings, fidgeted with the sash of his robe.

The silence stretched on, broken only by the ticking of an antique clock somewhere down the hall.

GUARDIAN FOR HIRE

The sheer force of Anna's presence seemed to create its own field of gravity.

But the prince summoned some bluster, some anger, and he puffed out his chest.

"Who do you think you are?" Prince Abarim finally spluttered, his voice cracking. He drew himself up to his full height, attempting to regain his composure. The emeralds on his collar caught the light as he straightened. "This is my palace. My country. You are nothing but a guest here, and you would do well to remember that."

Anna's smile never wavered, though her eyes grew colder. "You're right. I am a guest." She took a step forward into the hallway, forcing the prince to take an involuntary step back. "And where I come from, guests are treated with respect. As are their family members."

The prince's face flushed again, color rising from his neck to his hairline. One of the guards—the youngest of the four, with a thin mustache and anxious eyes—reached for his weapon.

Anna's gaze flicked to him, pinning him with a look that froze him mid-motion. "I wouldn't," she said simply.

The guard's hand stilled, hovering uncertainly above his holster. The smooth ceiling above reflected his indecision, the painted cherubs seeming to watch the scene with morbid fascination.

Anna turned her attention back to the prince. "Now, I believe it's quite late. My sister needs her rest. Perhaps we could continue this conversation at a more appropriate time? Say, never?"

For a moment, rage contorted Abarim's features, twisting his handsome face into something ugly and primal. The veins in his neck bulged, pulsing beneath his skin like worms beneath silk. His hands clenched into fists, heavy rings digging into his flesh.

Then, as quickly as it had appeared, the rage vanished, replaced by a mask of calculation. A smile spread across his face, not reaching his eyes, which remained hard and reptilian.

"Of course," he said, his voice smooth. "How thoughtless of me to disturb your sister's slumber. Please, accept my most sincere apologies."

He bowed, a courtly gesture at odds with the menace emanating from him. The motion sent light dancing across the embroidered falcon on his breast pocket, its thread seeming to shimmer with life.

"I do hope this... misunderstanding won't affect our business arrangement. After all, we have the falconry exhibition soon. So many important people will be in attendance." His eyes gleamed dangerously. "It would be a shame if anything were to go... awry."

Anna didn't care in the least. She'd faced far, far worse than this small man hiding in his father's shadow.

"Just one more thing," Anna said. "I need you to swear in front of your men that you'll leave my sister alone."

For a moment, she thought he might comply... but then she saw his eyes narrow. His pride seemed to realize that his men were watching.

Prince Abarim's face twisted into a sneer. "I will do no such thing. Your sister, like everything else in this palace, belongs to me. I'll do with her as I please."

For a second, Anna remained perfectly still, her expression placid. "Just remember," she whispered.

"Anna," Beth tried to interrupt from behind her.

Anna ignored her sister. "Remember, I tried to give you a chance. I really, really did."

They were in a foreign, hostile nation, facing one of the most powerful men in this prison state. They were surrounded by guards, military threats on all sides.

This, Anna supposed, was why the would-be prince felt so confident in his position. He thought he held all the cards.

But in playing cards, one has to know the rules, and Anna wasn't the type to play well with others.

This asshole had threatened her sister. She'd given him a chance, and he'd done it again.

Though to be honest, she would've handled him later that night. He'd sealed his fate the moment he'd knocked on Beth's door. Some called her the Guardian Angel...

But others?

Others knew her *better.* They referred to her only as the angel of death.

Anna exploded into motion.

Her hand shot out, snatching the letter opener from the nearby writing desk. The scimitar-shaped blade glinted.

The first guard barely had time to look up before the makeshift weapon slashed across his throat. A red line appeared, quickly turning into a crimson waterfall. He clutched at his neck, gurgling, as he crumpled to the floor.

Anna was already moving to the next target. The second guard managed to draw his pistol, but Anna was faster. The letter opener plunged into his eye socket with a sickening squelch. He screamed, the sound cut short as Anna wrenched the blade free, taking half his face with it.

The two remaining guards fumbled for their weapons, fingers slipping on holster clasps. Anna ducked under a wild swing, driving the letter opener up under the third guard's chin. The tip burst through the top of his skull in a spray of bone and brain matter.

As the final guard raised his gun, Anna hurled the blood-slick letter opener. It spun through the air, burying itself in the man's throat. He fired reflexively, the bullet going wide and shattering an antique vase. Flowers and water spilled across the floor, mingling with the spreading pools of blood.

Prince Abarim opened his mouth to scream for help, but Anna's fist crashed into his windpipe. The cry died in his throat, replaced by a strangled wheeze. He staggered back, eyes bulging, clawing at his neck.

The entire sequence had taken less than ten seconds.

Anna stood amid the carnage, her chest rising and falling steadily. Spatters of blood marred her face and clothes, droplets sliding down her skin like tears. The scent of copper filled the air.

Anna released an exhale and rolled her shoulders as if after a morning jog. She could hear her sister hyperventilating behind her.

Anna winced, glancing back.

Beth stared at the scene, her breath coming in short, rapid gasps. The hallway, once a show of wealth and power, now resembled a slaughterhouse. The walls, adorned with valuable artwork, were now splattered with gore, abstract patterns marring the delicate brushstrokes of long-dead masters.

Beth's eyes darted frantically from one fallen guard to another, taking in the gruesome details of their final moments. One man's face was frozen in a permanent scream, his remaining eye disfigured with terror. Another lay sprawled across a delicate end table, his outstretched hand having knocked over a porcelain figurine. The shepherdess now lay in pieces, her painted smile a mockery of the death surrounding her.

"You... you killed them," Beth whispered, her voice barely audible over the sound of her own frantic breathing. Her legs threatened to give way beneath her.

Anna turned to her sister, her expression impassive. Blood dripped from her fingertips, pattering softly to the ground. "You wanted to come," she said, her tone matter-of-fact. "Now help me with them."

Before Beth could respond, Anna moved to the prince, who lay groaning on the floor. With a swift, precise movement, she struck him at the base of the skull. His eyes rolled back, and he slumped into unconsciousness.

"Grab his feet," Anna instructed, already moving to lift the prince's shoulders.

Beth hesitated, her eyes wide with shock and disbelief. The prince's robe had fallen open, revealing a soft, pampered body at odds with the violence around him. A small golden key hung from a chain around his neck, rising and falling with each shallow breath.

"Beth," Anna's voice cut through her sister's daze. "Now."

Moving as if in a trance, Beth grasped the prince's ankles. Together, they dragged him into the bedroom, leaving a smear of blood across the threshold. The prince's head lolled listlessly, his carefully coiffed hair now matted with blood.

Once inside, Anna efficiently stripped the sheets from the bed, using them to bind the prince's hands and feet. The fine silk tore easily in her grip, the delicate fabric wholly unsuited for its new purpose.

"Tie him up," Anna ordered, tossing the makeshift bonds to her sister. "Make it tight. I'll get the others."

Beth fumbled with the knots, her hands slick with nervous sweat. She struggled to tighten the silk bonds around the prince's wrists and ankles, the fabric slipping through her fingers.

"I... I can't," she whispered, her voice cracking. "Anna, I can't do this."

Anna paused in the doorway, her expression softening slightly as she looked at her sister. For a moment, the hardened operative facade cracked, revealing a glimpse of the protective older sibling beneath.

"Yes, you can," Anna said firmly but gently. "You have to. We don't have much time."

She checked her watch. Seven minutes left. She had to hurry.

Anna worked swiftly, her movements purposeful. She dragged the fallen guards into the room one by one, their limp bodies leaving crimson trails across the marble floor.

As she hauled the last guard inside, Anna paused to survey the scene. Blood had seeped into the intricate patterns of a Persian carpet, turning its vibrant colors into a muddy crimson. Without hesitation, she rolled the rug up, concealing the worst of the carnage beneath its folds. The remaining blood spatters on the walls resembled abstract paintings against the pale wallpaper.

Anna grabbed a chair, its velvet upholstery now stained. She wedged it under the door handle, creating a makeshift barricade. The chair's legs scraped against the floor, leaving faint scratches that seemed to glow in the dim light.

"Listen carefully," Anna said, turning to Beth. Her sister sat on the edge of the bed, her face pale and drawn in the moonlight. "You need to come with me. I'm taking you to Waldo. He can keep an eye on you."

Beth sat frozen.

"You can't stay here," Anna insisted.

It took her sister a moment, but then Beth exhaled shakily and nodded. There was a time when it might have taken thirty minutes to calm her sister down. But even Beth, the stay-at-home mom turned covert operator, was growing tougher skin.

Anna frowned. She wasn't sure this was a good thing at all.

But she shoved the unconscious prince under the bed. "Insurance," she muttered.

Then, she led Beth to the balcony.

"We need to move," she whispered. "Don't slow down. Just follow me. You'll be fine, I promise."

Beth let out a slow whimper but nodded again, her expression resolute. "W-won't they find the blood?"

"Probably," Anna said. "But the prince waved the guards in the garden off. I'd guess we have an hour or so."

She didn't add *why* the prince had wanted witnesses to the east wing gone. She doubted it was the first time the deviant had tried to take advantage of his female guests.

They had time. Not much. But *some.* An hour? Two?

Eventually, the prince would be missed.

Two hours, Anna decided. Two hours before someone came to investigate the missing prince.

And that was if they were lucky.

She hurried to the edge of the railing, checking her watch.

Only a few minutes to meet up with Casper at the motor pool.

"Come on," she whispered. "We have to hurry."

Chapter 17

Anna sat in the front passenger seat of the slick black limousine as it pulled through the gates. Casper still wore the guard's uniform he'd stolen, but he kept shooting angry glances at Anna.

"Took your sweet time," he muttered under his breath. "The guard I bribed was almost off shift."

"Yeah, well... I made it," Anna whispered.

"Late."

"Barely," she replied. "Besides, I needed to make sure Beth was safe with Waldo."

"No one's safe with Waldo."

"You know what I mean."

Casper sighed, running a hand wearily through his cropped hair as they drove away from the compound. The guard who'd let them through was looking in any direction except the vehicle he'd just allowed to pass, as if by looking somewhere else, he wouldn't be responsible for the sizable bribe he'd just accepted.

"You have blood on your sleeve," Casper said, steering the vehicle away from the grounds.

"Where are we going?" Anna asked, side-stepping the comment.

Casper's jaw clenched as he navigated the sleek limousine through the empty streets of Ashgabat. The city at night was quiet, its wide boulevards deserted save for the occasional patrol vehicle.

"Industrial district on the outskirts of town," he replied tersely. "Our intel suggests the Albino has a safehouse there. It's our best lead on finding him and getting the information about Beth's family."

Anna nodded, her gaze scanning their surroundings. The gleaming white marble buildings gave way to more utilitarian structures as they left the city center. Factories and warehouses loomed in the darkness, their blank facades revealing nothing of what lay within.

"You want to tell me what happened back there?" Casper asked, breaking the silence. "Why you were late?"

Anna's expression remained neutral. "Complications arose. I handled them."

Casper snorted. "Handled them? Is that what we're calling it now?" He shook his head. "Anna, we can't afford to leave a trail of bodies behind us. Not here. Not when we're this close to our goal."

"It was necessary," Anna replied coolly. "The prince was a threat. I neutralized him."

"The *prince*, Anna," Casper muttered. "You can't just—"

"I can and I did," she interrupted. "He threatened Beth. That's all I needed to know."

Casper fell silent, recognizing the grit in her voice. He'd seen this side of Anna before, during their time in the SEALs. The utterly ruthless operative who would do whatever it took to complete the mission and protect her own.

As they approached the industrial zone, Anna checked her weapons one last time. The familiar weight of her pistol was comforting against her hip. She'd procured a few extra items from Waldo's armory before they left—a compact submachine gun now lay concealed beneath her jacket, and a set of ceramic throwing knives was strapped to her forearm.

"We're here," Casper announced, pulling the limo into a shadowy alley between two abandoned warehouses. The smell of rust and stagnant water filled the air.

Anna stepped out of the vehicle, her senses on high alert.

"Trap?" she whispered to Casper as he joined her.

He nodded grimly. "Almost certainly. But it's our only play."

Anna's lips curved into a predatory smile. "Then let's spring it. Got Waldo's trinket?"

Casper nodded again, pulling a silver suitcase out of the trunk. He placed it on the muddy asphalt, clicking the locks open.

Anna watched, forcing herself not to worry about her sister. So far, no news was good news.

She'd estimated two hours before people started looking for the prince. They had time.

But not much.

Casper flipped open the suitcase, revealing a matte-black drone nestled in custom-cut foam. Its carbon fiber body gleamed faintly in the dim light, four propellers folded neatly against its frame. A high-resolution camera was mounted on its underside, its lens catching what little light filtered into the alley.

As Casper began the preflight checks, Waldo's voice crackled to life in their earpieces.

"Ah, I see you've unveiled my masterpiece," Waldo said, his tone dripping with self-satisfaction. "The Nighthawk 3000. Top of the line, cutting edge, and if I do say so myself, a work of pure genius."

Anna rolled her eyes, her finger hovering over the mute button on her comm unit.

Undeterred by her faint sigh, Waldo continued, "This beauty can reach speeds of up to seventy miles per hour, has a flight time of forty-five minutes, and comes equipped with thermal imaging capabilities that would make the Pentagon envious. The carbon fiber frame is virtually undetectable by radar, and the noise-canceling technology means it's quieter than a church mouse with laryngitis."

As Waldo launched into a detailed explanation of the drone's proprietary encryption system, Anna finally hit the mute button, silencing the stream of technical jargon.

Casper smirked, powering up the drone. Its propellers unfolded with a whir, barely making a sound even in the quiet alley.

The camera lens adjusted, focusing on their faces for a moment before Casper directed it upward.

"He does love his toys," Casper muttered, guiding the drone into the air.

The Nighthawk 3000 rose silently, quickly disappearing into the blackness above. On the control pad, a crystal-clear image of the industrial zone from above began to form. Abandoned warehouses and rusting machinery created a maze of dark shapes and hidden corners.

Anna studied the thermal imaging display, her eyes searching for any signs of life. Most of the buildings showed up as cool blues and greens, their interiors long since abandoned to the elements.

"Is Beth there?" Anna asked finally, unmuting the comms.

"Your sister is fine. Reading a book on the couch," Waldo replied. "She's nicer than you. Prettier too. Just figured I should mention it."

"Thanks, Waldo. Appreciate that. I'll remind you just how much nicer she is next time I'm in a room with you, Strange."

A faint chuckle. "Ah, hang on," Waldo interrupted himself. "See that?"

Anna and Casper both stared at the screen between them.

Near the center, a structure caught her attention. Unlike its neighbors, this building glowed with the warm reds and yellows of recent human activity. Several heat signatures moved within, their patterns suggesting armed guards on patrol.

"There," Anna said, pointing to the anomaly. "That's got to be it."

Casper zoomed in on the target building. The drone's camera revealed a nondescript warehouse, its exterior weathered and unremarkable. But the thermal imaging told a different story—beneath that front lay a hive of activity.

"Looks like we've found our Albino's hideout," Casper murmured.

"Byers gave you the intel for the location?"

A nod from her partner. "Confirmed," he added. "My own boots on the ground. If he's here, then this is where."

Anna felt a thrill of excitement. "He's going to have a lot of firepower."

"Most definitely."

She studied the thermal imagery, already formulating a plan of attack. The warehouse was a fortress, but every fortress had its weak points. She just had to find them.

"Waldo, can you get us a more detailed scan of the building's interior?" she asked.

"Can I get a more detailed scan? Is the pope Catholic? Does a bear sh—"

"Just do it," Anna snapped, cutting off Waldo's colorful analogies.

The drone descended, hovering closer to the building. Its advanced sensors penetrated the warehouse's exterior, revealing a complex network of rooms and corridors within.

"Looks like we've got at least a dozen heat signatures inside," Casper observed, his voice low. "Probably more. They're well-armed too—I'm picking up weapon signatures consistent with assault rifles and possibly even some heavier ordinance."

Anna nodded grimly. "Any sign of our target?"

Casper manipulated the controls, scanning each room methodically. "There," he said finally, pointing to a heat signature in what appeared to be a central office. "That's got to be him. The way the others are positioned around him, he's clearly the VIP."

Anna leaned in, studying the figure. Even through the thermal imaging, there was something distinctly unsettling about the way the figure moved—a predatory air that set him apart from his guards.

"Alright," she said, straightening up. "We go in quiet. Two-pronged approach. I'll take the roof, you come in through the loading bay. We meet in the middle and take him together."

Casper raised an eyebrow. "That's a lot of hostiles to go through."

Anna shrugged, her eyes still fixed on the thermal imagery. "We've faced worse odds. Remember Kandahar? Or that time in Mogadishu when—"

"Guys, hold up!" Waldo's frantic voice crackled through their earpieces, interrupting Anna mid-sentence. "We've got a problem. A big one."

Anna and Casper exchanged worried glances. "What is it, Waldo?" Casper asked, his finger hovering over the drone's controls.

"The roof," Waldo said, his words tumbling out in a rush. "It's covered in sensors. High-tech stuff. Motion detectors, infrared cameras, the works. And they're active. They've already picked up the drone's presence."

Anna's blood ran cold. She looked up at the night sky, half expecting to see a swarm of missiles descending on them. But the alley remained quiet, for now.

"That's not all," Waldo continued, his voice rising in pitch. "I've detected sniper nests on the surrounding buildings. At least three, maybe more. They've got clear lines of sight to every approach. And... oh hell."

"What?" Anna demanded, her hand instinctively moving to her pistol.

"Facial recognition cameras at every entrance. The moment you step into view, they'll know exactly who you are... What the hell is this place? I've seen presidents with less protection."

Casper swore under his breath. "It's a goddamn fortress."

Anna's mind raced, processing this new information. The warehouse walls seemed to mock them, hiding layers upon layers of lethal security.

"We need to abort," Casper said, already reaching for the drone's controls. "Find another way."

But Anna hesitated, her eyes still focused on the thermal image of the figure in the central office. So close, yet impossibly far. The Albino was their only lead on Beth's missing family. To turn back now...

"Anna," Waldo's voice came through. "Listen to me. This place... it's not just secure. It's overkill. The kind of setup you'd use if you were expecting a small army, not a couple of operatives. Whatever's going on in there, it's bigger than we thought. Much bigger."

The weight of Waldo's words settled over them. The quiet alley suddenly felt exposed, vulnerable. Every shadow might hide potential threats.

"Okay," Anna said finally, her voice tight. "We pull back. Regroup and reassess."

As Casper began guiding the drone back to their position, Anna took a final look at the thermal scan.

She frowned at the central figure.

No telling if this was the Albino.

No telling if the intel they'd received was reliable at all. She let out a slow breath.

They needed to speak to their billionaire pal. If anyone might be able to shift the balance of power, it was him.

Besides, the job wasn't done until they got their hands on his Silver Falcon.

Casper was shaking his head, grumbling under his breath, likely thinking the same thing.

The prince was tied up under Beth's bed back at the palace. Four of his guards were dead.

Their one hope had been a quick exfil, but now... If they had to regroup, how were they supposed to handle the palace security?

They quickly packed up the drone and slipped back into the limousine. The enormity of their situation was settling in—they were trapped in a hostile nation, their only lead on Beth's family now seemingly unreachable, and a trail of bodies left behind at the palace. The clock was ticking.

As Casper navigated the empty streets back toward the city center, Anna's fingers drummed restlessly on her thigh. She needed a new plan, and fast.

"We can't stay at the palace," she said, breaking the silence. "It's only a matter of time before they find the prince and his guards."

"We can't leave the palace," Casper replied just as firmly.

"Don't see any options."

"Let me talk to him."

"Who? The prince?"

"Yeah. Let me talk to him." Casper eyed her. "He *is* still alive, isn't he?"

"And what is talking to him going to do? I killed four of his men and humiliated him."

"Yeah, but you also scared him. Guards are expendable. The prince? He isn't. I've turned assets before."

"CIA work?"

"It's a play," Casper insisted.

Anna considered Casper's suggestion, weighing the risks and potential benefits. The prince was a wild card—dangerous, unpredictable, but also potentially valuable. If they could turn him...

"Alright," she said finally, her voice terse. "We'll try it your way. But if he doesn't cooperate, we move to plan B."

Casper grimaced, understanding the unspoken implication. Plan B would be messy, violent, and likely end with more bodies.

As they approached the palace, Anna watched the grounds for any signs of alarm or increased security. So far, everything appeared normal—the same lush gardens, the same patrols moving in their regular patterns. Their window of opportunity was still open, but for how long?

Chapter 18

Back in Beth's room, the air was putrid with the sickly-sweet stench of death. The once lavish chamber had been transformed into a makeshift morgue. Moonlight filtered through the window, casting long shadows across the blood-stained carpet.

Anna stood in the corner, her back pressed against the cool wall. Her eyes, sharp and alert, never left the scene unfolding before her.

Casper, his face obscured by a black balaclava, bent down and grasped the bed skirt. The moment he reached under the bed, a voice started grunting and protesting.

Casper dragged the bound and gagged Prince Abarim out from under the bed. The prince's formerly immaculate silk robe was now torn and stained with blood, his carefully coiffed hair matted and disheveled. His eyes darted wildly around the room, widening in horror as they fell on the bodies of his guards.

Anna watched impassively as Casper hauled the prince into a sitting position, propping him against the foot of the bed. With a swift motion, Casper removed the gag, allowing Abarim to draw in a ragged breath.

"You... you'll pay for this," the prince sputtered, his voice hoarse. "Do you have any idea who I am? What my uncle will do to you when he finds out?"

Casper crouched down, bringing his face level with the prince's. "That's exactly what we're here to discuss, your highness," he said, his tone measured. "Your future. And ours."

The prince's eyes narrowed, a flicker of calculation replacing the fear. "What do you want?" he asked, his voice steadier.

Casper leaned in closer, his voice dropping to a menacing whisper. "What we want is your cooperation. And in return, we offer you something far more valuable than money or power. We offer you survival."

The prince's brow furrowed, confusion and disbelief warring on his face. The ornate tapestry behind him, depicting an ancient battle scene, seemed to mock his current predicament.

Its woven warriors, frozen in eternal combat, loomed over the prince like silent judges.

"You see," Casper continued, his eyes never leaving Abarim's face, "we know all about your... extracurricular activities. The parties at your private villa on the Caspian. The girls you've had brought in from the poorest villages. The way you use your position to satisfy your most depraved desires."

Anna blinked. She knew Casper came prepared on missions, but this was all news to her.

She studied Abarim's expression. The veracity was written all over his countenance.

His face drained of color, his skin taking on an ashen hue. A drop of sweat trickled down his temple, catching the moonlight.

"That's... that's a pack of lies," he stammered, but his voice lacked conviction. "Propaganda spread by my enemies."

Casper's laugh was harsh and humorless. "Oh, we have more than just rumors. We have evidence. Photos. Videos. Testimony from some of your victims. Including your own cousin, Amina."

At the mention of his cousin's name, Abarim flinched as if struck. His eyes darted to the window, perhaps seeking escape, but found only his own reflection staring back at him—disheveled, bound, and utterly powerless.

"Amina would never..." he began, but Casper cut him off.

"She already has. In excruciating detail. About how you cornered her at the family gathering last Ramadan. How you threatened to have her father's business licenses revoked if she didn't comply with your demands. How you—"

"Enough!" Abarim shouted, his voice cracking. "What do you want from me?"

Casper paused, letting the weight of the moment settle over the room. The antique clock on the mantle ticked steadily, each second marking the prince's dwindling options.

"What we want," Casper said slowly, "is for you to understand the precariousness of your position. Your uncle, the general—how do you think he'd react if this information came to light? A man of his standing, his devotion to tradition and family honor?"

Abarim's face contorted in rage. "My uncle would never believe—"

"He wouldn't have to believe," Casper interrupted. "The evidence speaks for itself. And even if he had doubts, could he afford to take that risk? A scandal of this magnitude..." Casper trailed off, making a clicking noise with his tongue.

The prince's eyes darted between Anna and Casper, calculating his odds. The room seemed like a cage now, the gilded furniture and crystal chandeliers trappings for what had become his prison. The bodies of his guards lay sprawled nearby, reminders of how quickly his world could fall apart.

"What exactly do you want from me?" Abarim finally asked, his voice sounding defeated. The golden key around his neck caught the moonlight as his chest rose and fell with rapid breaths.

Casper leaned back slightly, giving the prince room to breathe. "It's quite simple, really. You will continue to host us as your honored guests. You will ensure that no one discovers what happened here tonight."

His eyes hardened. "But first, you're going to make a little video for us."

He pulled out a smartphone, its screen glowing in the dimness of the room. The prince's eyes widened as Casper aimed the camera at him.

"What... what are you doing?" Abarim stammered, shrinking back against the bed.

"Insurance," Casper replied coolly. He glanced at Anna, who nodded and stepped forward, drawing her pistol in one quick motion. The silencer at the end of the barrel glinted dully in the moonlight.

Anna pressed the muzzle of the gun against the prince's temple. The metal made him flinch, a whimper escaping his lips.

"Now," Casper said, his finger hovering over the record button, "you're going to confess everything to your uncle. In detail."

"I... I can't," the prince pleaded, his eyes moving between the gun and the camera. "He'll kill me."

"That's a possibility," Casper agreed. "But it's also possible he'll simply exile you. Strip you of your titles, your wealth. But you'll be alive. Or maybe he'll stage a coup against your father. Maybe even hire an assassin." He paused, letting the words sink in. "If you don't do this, however... Well, my colleague here isn't known for her patience."

As if to emphasize the point, Anna pressed the gun harder against the prince's head. A trail of sweat traced his temple, following the contours of the pistol's barrel.

The mirrors on the walls reflected the scene from multiple angles—the tied-up prince, the looming figures of Anna and

Casper, the bodies of the fallen guards just visible at the edge of the frame.

For a long moment, the room was silent except for the prince's erratic breathing. Outside, the palace grounds remained quiet, but Anna knew it wouldn't last. Someone would come looking for the prince eventually.

"Fine," Abarim finally said, his voice barely audible. "I'll do it."

Casper nodded and pressed record. "Whenever you're ready, your highness."

The prince swallowed hard, his Adam's apple bobbing beneath the thin skin of his throat. When he spoke, his voice trembled with a mixture of fear and self-preservation.

"Uncle," he began, his eyes fixed on the camera lens, "I have committed acts that bring shame to our family and our nation." The words seemed to physically pain him, each one dragged reluctantly from his lips. "I have... I have used my position to coerce..."

As the confession continued, growing more detailed and damning with each passing minute, Anna watched the prince's face. His aristocratic features, once haughty and imperious, now seemed small and pathetic. His expression grew more distraught as he enumerated his crimes.

When he fell silent, Casper stopped the recording and pocketed the phone. "Very good. Now, let's discuss your immediate future."

Anna lowered her weapon but remained vigilant. The prince's cooperation could be a ploy, a desperate man buying time until he could turn the tables. She'd seen it before—cornered animals were often the most dangerous.

"You will call the head of palace security," Casper instructed. "You will tell him there was an incident with some rowdy guests at your private party. You had to... discipline them. The bodies need to be disposed of quietly, and no record is to be made of tonight's events."

The prince nodded numbly, glancing at the corpses of his guards. "And after that?"

"After that, you become our ally," Casper said simply. "You provide us with information, access, whatever we need to complete our mission. In return, this recording remains our little secret."

Abarim grimaced, a flicker of his former arrogance returning. "And if I refuse? If I call your bluff?"

Anna stepped forward, her movement so sudden that the prince recoiled. She crouched down, bringing her face level with his. Her green eyes bored into him, uncompromising.

"Then I finish what I started," she said firmly. "But not before I send that recording to every media outlet from here to Washington. Your uncle might kill you quickly. The angry fathers and brothers of the women you've abused? They'll take their time."

The prince blanched, all traces of defiance evaporating. "I understand," he replied.

Casper untied the prince's hands cautiously. "Make the call," he said, handing Abarim a satellite phone. "And remember, we're listening to every word."

The prince's fingers shook as he dialed, leaving smudges on the phone's glossy surface. When the head of security answered, Abarim's voice transformed, adopting a tone of command.

"There's been an incident in the east wing," he said, the words clipped and authoritative. "Four of my personal guards. Yes, that's right. No, no authorities. This is a private matter. Send your most discreet team." He paused, listening. "I don't care how you do it. Just make it happen. And Fareed? If word of this reaches my uncle..." He left the threat hanging, his eyes flicking to Anna.

As he ended the call, some of the tension drained from his shoulders. "It's done," he said. "They'll be here in twenty minutes."

"Good," Casper replied, retrieving the phone. "Now, about our mutual arrangement. We need information about the Albino."

The prince's head snapped up, his eyes showing genuine surprise. "The arms dealer? What could you possibly want with him?"

"That's our business," Anna interjected. "Just tell us what you know."

Abarim shifted uncomfortably, the silk of his torn robe rustling against the carpet. "He's not someone you want to cross. Even in Turkmenistan, there are those who fear him."

"We're not looking to cross him," Casper said smoothly. "Just to have a conversation."

The prince laughed, a brittle sound. "A conversation? With the Albino? You might as well try to have a conversation with a scorpion before it stings you."

Anna's patience was wearing thin. "The warehouse in the industrial district. Is he there?"

Abarim's brow furrowed. "Warehouse? No, no. The Albino would never operate from somewhere so... crude. He has a compound in the desert, about fifty miles east of the city. A fortress, really. Built during the Soviet era as a nuclear research facility."

Anna and Casper exchanged a look. This contradicted their intelligence from Byers. Either the prince was lying, or someone had fed them false information.

"You're sure about this?" Casper pressed.

The prince nodded vigorously. "Absolutely. I've been there myself, for... business dealings. The security is impenetrable. Razor wire, motion sensors, armed guards. He even has his own private army."

"Who would be at the industrial district, then?" Casper asked, frowning.

Abarim shrugged. "A decoy? I don't know. But not the Albino... not unless." A frown.

"Unless?"

"Unless someone has him running scared." The prince's gaze landed on Anna. "If he knows someone is after him..." A pause. "Maybe he's moved... temporarily."

Anna scowled at the ground for a moment, then looked up again. The prince was still eyeing both of them, and she could see his mind moving fast. If anyone was a scorpion, it was him.

This was a temporary band-aid. The prince wouldn't take kindly to any of this. The wound to his pride would likely hurt more than the deaths of his guards.

No. They'd have to move fast.

Anna nudged Casper. The two of them began to back away.

If the Albino was at a separate compound, then Byers—the man who'd hired them—was wrong. If he was at the industrial district, then something had him spooked. Did he know Anna was here?

She released a pent-up breath. They needed to lure the Albino out. If they could get him to a *known,* less protected location, then they'd have access.

On top of that, this palace and prince were a ticking time bomb.

Casper held up his phone with the video recording. He pointed at the prince. "We're watching," he murmured.

And then he turned and slipped away, Anna following.

Chapter 19

Anna felt a wave of relief every time she glanced toward her sister. Beth sat at the edge of Waldo's bed where the hacker had set up a temporary command center in their guest quarters. Waldo's empty luggage was splayed across the floor, serving as temporary tables.

Multiple screens displayed various feeds: thermal imaging of the palace grounds, security camera loops, and satellite imagery of both the industrial district and the desert compound the prince had mentioned. Cables snaked across the floor, connecting an array of devices whose purposes Anna could only guess at.

Waldo hunched over a keyboard, his fingers flying across the keys with manic energy. The blue glow of the screens cast harsh lines across his weasel-like features, making him appear even more untrustworthy than usual.

"So let me get this straight," Waldo said without looking up from his work. "You managed to piss off one of the most powerful men in Turkmenistan, kill four of his guards, and now you're blackmailing him with a confession tape?" He let out a low whistle. "And I thought I had impulse control issues."

Anna ignored the jab, focusing instead on the thermal scan of the desert compound. "Can you get us a better look at this place?"

Waldo rolled his eyes but complied, his fingers tapping away on the keyboard. The satellite image zoomed in, revealing more details of the Soviet-era facility. A high perimeter fence surrounded a cluster of concrete buildings. Guard towers dotted the landscape, and what appeared to be minefields stretched out in all directions.

"Charming vacation spot," Casper muttered, studying the image over Anna's shoulder.

"The blackmailee—that's a word, right? He wasn't kidding about the security. And that's just what we can see from space," Waldo added. "God knows what kind of surprises are waiting inside."

Beth, who had been quiet until now, finally spoke up. "Do you think he was telling the truth? About the Albino being there and not at the warehouse?"

Anna frowned, considering the question. "Hard to say. He had no reason to lie at that point, but..."

"But princes who've just been humiliated and forced to confess their crimes at gunpoint aren't known for their honesty," Casper finished for her. "We need to verify."

Waldo snorted. "Yeah, good luck with that. It's not like we can just call up the Albino and ask where he's hanging out these days."

A thoughtful expression crossed Anna's face. "Maybe we can." She frowned in concentration. "Or maybe... we don't need to go to him." Waldo, Beth, and Casper all turned to look at her.

There was the sound of movement outside their door. Waldo tensed, staring as someone passed by, but then the sounds from the hallway faded.

For now, they weren't being dragged off to a Turkmen prison... But who knew how long their luck would hold.

"We need to draw him out," Anna said with certainty. "Get the Albino to leave cover."

"But if he's spooked," Casper muttered, "Why would he ever do that?"

"Because," Anna replied. "We have something he wants." She paused, pacing back and forth. "At least... we know *he* has something our billionaire friend wants."

"The falcon," Waldo said, suddenly, staring at her. "The Golden Falcon of Nisa..."

"Exactly." Anna pointed at him. "If our billionaire bud wants the Silver Falcon so badly, as the second part of the key... then what are the odds that the Albino doesn't feel the same way about the Golden Falcon?" She shrugged. "Two halves of one key."

Casper whistled. "If it's as powerful as Atayev says it is, then the Albino would *definitely* want the second half. We need to find a location that he won't be too suspicious of."

Anna nodded. "The falconry exhibit. It's already a planned event. Been advertised for months. All the wealthy sorts will be there."

Waldo's eyes glinted as he caught on to Anna's plan. "Use the falconry exhibition as bait? That's... actually not terrible." His fingers flew across the keyboard, pulling up details of the upcoming event. "It's scheduled for tomorrow afternoon. All the local bigwigs will be there, including representatives from neighboring countries."

Anna shifted her stance, her thoughts racing ahead. "The perfect cover. We leak information that the Golden Falcon will be on display as part of the exhibition. The Albino won't be able to resist."

"And how exactly do we leak this information?" Casper asked, his tone skeptical. "It's not like we can take out an ad in the *Turkmenistan Daily*."

A predatory smile spread slowly across Anna's face. "We don't have to. The prince will do it for us."

Beth looked up abruptly. "The prince? After what you did to him?"

"Especially after what I did to him," Anna replied. "He's desperate to save his own skin now. If he thinks helping us will keep that confession video from reaching his uncle, he'll do whatever we ask."

Casper rubbed his chin thoughtfully. "It could work. The prince has the connections to spread the word in the right circles. And the Albino would be more likely to believe it coming from him than from an anonymous source."

Waldo leaned back in his chair, his face still illuminated by his screens. "So we get the prince to announce that the Golden Falcon will be displayed at tomorrow's exhibition. The Albino shows up, and then what? We grab him in front of half the Turkmen government?"

"We need the lights to go out," Anna said. "Chaos. Smoke. Mirrors. All of it."

Waldo sighed, scratching his nose. "I'm guessing that's where I come in."

"Yup."

"I'm staying here, though. Safe and sound."

"Sure," Anna said. "If you think the palace is safe after what we did." She shrugged. "Your call."

Waldo gnawed on his lower lip, then scowled at her. "I don't like you very much."

Anna smirked. "You say the sweetest things. But Casper—we need you to speak to Atayev."

"He's not going to loan us his beloved treasure."

"Tell him it's the only way to get the Silver Falcon."

"Is it?" Casper asked.

Anna nodded. "The Albino will bring his. If he buys the ruse, he'll want to make sure he's getting his hands on the authentic Golden Falcon."

"And you think having both in the room is the only way to do that?"

"They're two halves of a key, aren't they? It's a good bet. Besides, if we get our hands on the Albino, then we have access to his falcon."

"And if we don't?" Casper pressed.

"Let's not forget why we're actually here. If Atayev cuts us loose, we'll find our own way out."

Waldo tapped a series of commands into his computer, bringing up a 3D schematic of the exhibition hall. The holographic display hovered in the air, casting eerie light across their faces.

"The falconry exhibition is being held in the Grand Hall," he explained, zooming in on a section of the palace. "High ceilings, lots of open space, multiple entrances and exits. Security will be concentrated here, here, and here." His finger jabbed at various points around the perimeter.

Casper studied the layout, his expression grim. "Too many variables. Too many civilians. If this goes sideways..."

"It won't," Anna said confidently, though the tightness around her eyes betrayed her own concerns. "Not if we plan it right."

She moved to the window, peering out at the palace grounds. Dawn was approaching, the sky lightening to a pale lavender. Soon the palace would be bustling with activity as preparations for the exhibition began.

"Casper, talk to Atayev. Convince him that we need the Golden Falcon as bait. Waldo, I need you to find a way to cut power to the exhibition hall at my signal. And Beth..." Anna hesitated, turning to her sister.

Beth sat up straighter. "What do you need me to do?"

Anna studied her for a moment. The last thing she wanted was to put Beth in danger, but they needed all hands for this to work. More importantly, she needed Beth away from the rooms. Away from the prince. "You'll be my eyes in the crowd. Watch for the Albino, but don't engage. Just signal me when you spot him."

Beth gave her affirmation, her jaw set with resolve. The soft morning light highlighted the family resemblance between the sisters—the same determined jawline, the same intensity in their eyes.

"And what about the prince?" Casper asked. "How do we ensure he plays his part?"

Anna's lips curled. "Leave that to me."

"You're going to threaten him?" Waldo guessed.

Anna nodded. "I'm going to threaten him."

Chapter 20

The threatening part went without a hitch. The prince had fulfilled his role marvelously, and now, Anna watched as the event's venue was set up on the palace grounds.

The falconry exhibition had transformed the Grand Hall into a spectacle of exoticism. Massive golden cages housed birds of prey from across Central Asia—golden eagles with razor-sharp talons, peregrine falcons whose sleek bodies seemed designed for lethal speed, and the rare Turkmenistan desert hawk, its feathers the color of sand and blood.

The exhibition had drawn exactly the type of crowd they'd hoped for—government officials in their finest regalia, foreign dignitaries seeking to curry favor with Turkmenistan's reclusive regime, and wealthy collectors eager to glimpse the birds. The air buzzed with excited conversation in a dozen languages, the scent of expensive perfumes mingling with the musky odor of the captive falcons.

Anna spotted Beth across the hall, looking elegant yet understated in a simple blue dress. Her sister moved through the crowd with surprising grace, pausing occasionally to admire a particularly impressive bird or a spectacle. No one would suspect she was scanning faces, looking for their target.

Casper's voice crackled in Anna's earpiece. "Atayev is in position. He's not happy about using the Golden Falcon as bait, but he's cooperating."

Anna found the billionaire standing near the central display case that would soon house the ancient artifact. Atayev looked every inch the powerful oligarch—expensive suit, confident posture, surrounded by an entourage of assistants and security personnel. But Anna could see the strain in his shoulders, the tight grip he maintained on his walking stick.

"Good," she murmured, turning slightly to speak into the concealed microphone. "Waldo, are you ready with the power?"

"Ready as I'll ever be," Waldo replied, his voice tinged with his usual nervous energy. "One flip of a digital switch, and this place goes darker than my ex's heart."

Anna surveyed the room. Prince Abarim stood near the entrance, greeting guests with a fixed smile that didn't reach his eyes. When their gazes met briefly, Anna saw a flash of hatred so intense it was almost palpable. The prince quickly looked away, but the message was clear—he was playing along for now, but this wasn't over.

"Our princely friend is behaving himself," Anna noted quietly.

"For the time being," Casper responded. "Don't turn your back on him."

"Wasn't planning to," Anna replied, moving deeper into the crowd.

The exhibition was scheduled to begin in thirty minutes. According to the prince's "leaked" information, the Golden Falcon would be unveiled as the grand finale. If the Albino took the bait, he would make his move then.

A hush fell over the crowd as the lights dimmed, focusing attention on the central ring where the falconry demonstrations would take place. The ring itself was a masterpiece of design—a circular arena fifty feet in diameter, its floor covered in fine sand the color of pale gold. Intricate wooden perches of varying heights dotted the space, each one carved with scenes of ancient hunting parties.

The Falconer, a weathered Turkmen man whose face bore the deep lines of a lifetime spent in the harsh desert sun, strode into the ring. His traditional chapan coat, richly embroidered in crimson and gold, swept around his ankles as he moved. Leather gauntlets protected his forearms, their surfaces worn smooth from years of supporting the weight of hunting birds.

"Ladies and gentlemen," announced a voice in multiple languages over the sound system, "welcome to the Exhibition of the Royal Falcons of Turkmenistan."

The Falconer raised his arm, and a magnificent golden eagle descended from the rafters, its wingspan easily six feet across. The crowd gasped as the massive bird landed with surprising delicacy on the man's outstretched arm. Its feathers gleamed in the spotlight, its yellow eyes surveying the audience with imperial disdain.

With a series of whistles and hand gestures, the Falconer sent the eagle soaring around the arena. It flew with breathtaking ease, executing tight turns and dives that showcased its power and agility. At one point, it plummeted toward the ground at terrifying speed, pulling up at the last possible moment to snatch a small target from the sand.

Anna kept her focus split between the spectacle and the crowd. The exhibition was impressive, certainly, but it was merely the backdrop for their operation. She constantly scanned for unfamiliar faces, for anyone who might be the Albino or his operatives.

The demonstration continued as four handlers entered the ring, each carrying a different species of falcon on their arms. They formed a perfect square in the center, then, at a signal from the Falconer, released their birds simultaneously. The falcons shot upward in perfect synchronization, their wings catching the light as they spiraled toward the high ceiling.

What followed was a breathtaking aerial ballet. The birds wove around each other in complex patterns, never colliding, creating compositions in the air. The audience watched in awe as the falcons dived, soared, and pirouetted with precision, responding to subtle commands from their handlers below.

For the finale of this portion, a small drone was released into the arena. The crowd murmured in surprise as the mechanical intruder buzzed through the air. In an instant, all four falcons changed direction, converging on the drone with lethal intent. The lead bird, a peregrine falcon known for being the fastest animal on earth, struck first, its talons slashing through the drone's plastic shell. The other three followed, and within seconds, pieces of the drone were raining down onto the ground bel ow.

The audience erupted in applause. Anna used the distraction to check in with her team.

"Any sign of our target?" she asked into her concealed microphone.

"Nothing yet," Beth's voice came through, slightly tense. "What if... what if he doesn't come?"

"He will," Anna said.

"How... how can you be sure?"

Anna didn't reply.

She *wasn't* sure. But they'd run into the Albino before. He'd blown a helicopter out of the sky with an RPG. He'd planned the deaths of Beth's family members.

They still didn't know if those had been faked or not.

Everything counted on Beth's family still being alive. And the only person who could *tell* them that had been baited into coming to this exhibit.

Would he show?

Audacious. Greedy. Powerful.

"He has to," Anna said under her breath.

"East," Casper's voice suddenly echoed in her ear.

Anna casually turned her attention to the doorway Casper indicated. A group of late arrivals was entering—men in expensive suits, their movements confident and purposeful. At their center walked a figure who immediately drew Anna's attention.

He was tall and lean, with skin so pale it seemed almost translucent under the hall's bright lights. His hair, cut close to his scalp, was white as fresh snow, contrasting sharply with the black suit he wore. Dark sunglasses concealed his eyes, but Anna knew instinctively who he was.

"The Albino," she breathed. " Moving toward the central display."

"Confirmed," Casper replied. "I see him. Four bodyguards, possibly armed."

Anna studied their target as he moved through the crowd. There was something predatory about his movements, a deadly grace that reminded her of the falcons themselves. His head turned slightly, scanning the room with the efficiency of a seasoned operative.

"He's carrying a case," Beth observed, her voice barely audible over the ambient noise of the crowd. "Silver, attached to his wrist by a chain."

Anna's pulse quickened.

"Atayev has spotted him," Casper reported. "He's looking nervous."

Anna watched as the billionaire shifted his weight from foot to foot, his fingers drumming an anxious rhythm on his walking stick. The Golden Falcon was scheduled to be unveiled in less than ten minutes. Everything was falling into place.

"Waldo, stand by with the power cut," Anna instructed. "On my mark, not before."

"Standing by," Waldo confirmed. "Just say the word, and we'll be playing blindman's bluff with the Turkmen elite."

The master of ceremonies returned to the center of the arena, gesturing for silence. "Ladies and gentlemen, we now come to the highlight of our exhibition. A treasure of immeasurable historical and cultural significance, recently recovered after decades abroad. I present to you... the Golden Falcon of Nisa!"

A curtain was drawn back from the central display case, revealing... nothing.

A murmur of confusion rippled through the crowd. The display case stood empty, its velvet-lined interior conspicuously bare. The master of ceremonies blinked in confusion, looking frantically toward Prince Abarim, who appeared equally stunned.

Anna's hand moved instinctively to her concealed weapon. "Waldo, what's happening?"

"Don't ask me," Waldo's voice came through, genuinely surprised. "This wasn't part of the plan."

Anna looked to Atayev. The billionaire stood frozen, his face a mask of shock and anger. Whatever was happening, he clearly hadn't anticipated it either.

Then Anna spotted new movement near the east exit—the Albino was retreating, his bodyguards forming a protective barrier around him. His pale face betrayed no emotion, but his hasty departure spoke volumes.

"He's running," Anna hissed. "Casper, intercept. Waldo, hit the lights now!"

"On it," Waldo replied, and instantly the Grand Hall plunged into darkness.

Chaos erupted. The crowd's confused murmurs transformed into shouts of alarm. In the darkness, Anna moved with practiced care, navigating by memory and sound. The falcons, disturbed by the sudden noise, added to the confusion with their piercing cries.

Anna slipped through the panicking guests, heading toward the east exit where she'd last seen the Albino. Her eyes adjusted quickly, picking out shapes and movements. She could hear Casper's focused breathing through her earpiece as he converged on the same target.

"Beth, stay where you are," Anna commanded. "Don't move until the lights come back on."

A sudden flash of movement to her right—Anna ducked instinctively as something whistled past her ear. A knife embedded itself in the wall behind her with a solid *thunk*. She dropped into a crouch, scanning for the attacker.

A figure lunged from the shadows, another blade glinting in his hand. One of the Albino's bodyguards. Anna sidestepped the attack, grabbing the man's wrist and twisting sharply. The knife clattered to the floor as bones snapped with a resounding crack. Before he could cry out, Anna drove her elbow into his throat, crushing his larynx. He collapsed, gasping silently for air that wouldn't come.

"East corridor clear," Casper's voice reported in her ear. "No sign of the target. He's fast."

Anna continued toward the exit, stepping over the fallen bodyguard. "He's heading for the garage. Cut him off at the south entrance."

Emergency lights flickered on across the hall. In their dim glow, Anna could see the aftermath of the power cut—guests huddled against walls, security personnel rushing in all directions, the falcons pulling against their restraints, agitated by the disturbance.

Where had the billionaire's falcon gone? There'd only been a small window when security would've deposited the golden falcon in the display case.

Had someone intercepted it?

The Albino? Possibly. But why would he have shown up if he'd intended to steal the thing before it had even reached the display?

One of the prince's men?

Also possible.

She cursed under her breath. "Unlikely..."

Then who?

"Casper... eyes out for a third party," she said. "We might've attracted more attention than I'd anticipated."

"Roger," Casper said. "Hang tight. Don't leave the arena."

But Anna spotted the Albino slipping out the main entrance with his security team. The window for apprehending him was closing.

"Negative," she said. "Moving. Provide overwatch."

"Damn... Anna!" snapped Casper. "Wait—Anna!"

But she was already in motion. No time to hesitate. She burst through a throng of befuddled guests, using classic SEAL "penetration" movement—maintaining a forward lean, arms in tight, hands up near chest level to create a wedge, and staying light on the balls of her feet. The stance allowed her to slide between panicked guests with minimal contact while maintaining her momentum.

She tracked the Albino's path, mentally figuring out where to intercept him. The exhibition hall's vaulted ceiling amplified the sounds of confusion—screams, footfalls, the agitated screeches of falcons still in their cages.

Anna identified a service corridor that ran parallel to the main hallway. Standard palace architecture meant it would likely connect to the same exit point but with fewer obstacles. She slipped through an unmarked door, finding herself in a narrow passage used by palace staff. The tactical advantage was immediate—clear sightlines, no civilians, and a straight shot to the south wing.

She moved in a modified CQB stance—weapon drawn but low, shoulders squared to potential threats, maintaining what SEALs called the "fatal funnel awareness" as she approached each intersection. Her steps were deliberately placed heel-to-toe to minimize noise, a technique she'd perfected during night operations in Fallujah.

"Switching to alternate route, service corridor alpha," she subvocalized into her comm. "Casper, what's your position?"

"South entrance, external perimeter," came the reply. "Target is moving toward vehicle staging area. Four-vehicle convoy, armored SUVs, professional security formation."

Anna processed this information. A four-vehicle motorcade meant serious protection—typically lead vehicle, principal vehicle, follow vehicle, and rear security. The formation would allow for contingency maneuvers like the "J-turn" or "reverse diamond" if threatened.

She needed to intercept before they formed up.

Anna reached a junction in the corridor and paused, pressing her back against the wall. She performed a quick sensory check—a three-second drill ingrained from countless operations. She regulated her breathing, controlled her heart rate, and listened beyond the chaos. The distinct sound of combat boots on marble came from her right—security personnel, moving fast.

She checked her weapon—a suppressed H&K P30 with subsonic 9mm rounds. Full magazine, round chambered, safety off. The weapon was chosen specifically for this operation—reliable in close quarters, minimal overpenetration risk, and effective terminal ballistics against unarmored targets.

Anna made a tactical decision. Direct pursuit would lead to a firefight in the open—unfavorable odds against multiple opponents with possible civilian casualties. Instead, she would utilize the palace infrastructure to her advantage.

"Waldo, I need a thermal scan of the south garage," she barked into her comm. "And cut power to the vehicle staging area."

"On it," Waldo replied. "Wait... Wait, Anna—hang on. Someone's out there... Someone on the roof."

Anna had been about to emerge onto the walkway to the garage, but at Waldo's warning, she hesitated.

This brief pause saved her life. A bullet clanged off the rail where she would've been standing if she hadn't stopped. Sparks erupted inches ahead off the steel partition.

Every instinct in her reacted at once, and she flung herself to the floor of the walkway, taking cover as her comms erupted into shouts of warning.

Chapter 21

Kovac whistled softly under his breath as he aimed for a second shot.

He lay prone on the rooftop of the palace's southern wing, his body a perfect horizontal line against the weathered copper. The position offered him unparalleled sightlines to the walkway connecting the main building to the garage structure. Heat rippled up from the metal surface, the afternoon sun having baked it to an uncomfortable temperature. He didn't notice. Discomfort was a distraction, and distractions were for amateurs.

The experimental rifle he'd acquired from Dmitri rested in his hands like an extension of his body. Its matte-black finish absorbed light rather than reflecting it, the barrel stabilized by a custom bipod that distributed weight evenly across the roofing surface. The scope—a military prototype with thermal overlay capabilities—displayed the heat signatures of everyone within range, their bodies glowing orange and yellow against the cooler blues and greens of the surrounding architecture.

"Angel moey smerti, ya zhdu tebya," Kovac whispered to himself. "Angel of my death, I wait for you."

He continued the poem he'd composed during the long nights spent tracking his prey.

"Your eyes, green as poison

Your hands, red with blood

We'll meet in the final dance

You and I, forever."

The words flowed from him as he made minute adjustments to the rifle's position. The weapon was unlike any he'd ever handled—its bullets contained gyroscopic micro-stabilizers that could be adjusted midflight via the targeting computer integrated into the scope. A small joystick near the trigger guard allowed for corrections of up to three feet in any direction, compensating for wind, movement, or miscalculation.

Kovac's finger hovered over the joystick as he tracked the thermal signature hidden behind the metal barrier of the walkway entrance. The Guardian Angel—Anna—was keeping low. Her heat signature burned brighter than those around her, as if her very blood ran hotter than normal humans.

His first shot had missed by millimeters. A warning, perhaps, from whatever god watched over assassins. Or simple bad luck—the wind had gusted unexpectedly just as he'd squeezed the trigger. It wouldn't happen again.

The rooftop was scattered with small pebbles and debris, each piece carefully examined and accounted for before he'd settled into position. Nothing that could roll unexpectedly or crunch underfoot. His black tactical suit blended in with the shadows of ventilation equipment, making him nearly invisible to casual observation. A coil of rope lay beside him, secured to a sturdy pipe—his extraction route already planned and prepared.

Kovac adjusted the scope's magnification, keeping Anna's heat signature in sight.

Next to him was a bag with the Golden Falcon... He'd seen through the Guardian's ruse easily enough. Two dead guards and two bribes had given him the brief access he'd needed.

Kovac had stolen the Golden Falcon just forty minutes earlier. The operation had been simple—intercept the artifact during the narrow transfer window between the secure vault and exhibition hall. The falcon had been scheduled for delivery at precisely 2:17 PM, moving through a staff corridor with only two guards as escorts. Kovac had timed it perfectly.

He'd entered the palace through the kitchen delivery entrance, wearing the uniform of a catering service he'd observed during reconnaissance. The kitchen staff, overwhelmed with exhibition preparations, barely glanced at another worker moving purposefully through their space. He carried a covered silver serving tray, identical to dozens of others being prepared for the elite guests.

At exactly 2:15 PM, Kovac had positioned himself in an alcove along the transfer corridor, seemingly becoming part of the architecture. When the guards appeared, along with a curator who carried a locked case, Kovac activated a small device in his pocket. Immediately, all radio communications within thirty meters experienced interference—not enough to trigger alarms, but sufficient to distract the guards who instinctively reached for their earpieces.

In that momentary lapse of attention, Kovac struck. A dart tipped with a fast-acting sedative found the curator's neck. As the man stumbled, Kovac's hands were a blur as he neutralized the first guard with a precise strike to the vagus nerve. The second guard managed to draw his weapon, but Kovac was faster, deflecting the gun hand upward while simultaneously delivering a crushing blow to the man's trachea.

The entire encounter had lasted less than four seconds. No sounds louder than a surprised gasp were made.

Kovac dragged the bodies into a nearby storage room, using zip ties to secure them should they regain consciousness. The case containing the Golden Falcon required three different keys—all of which the curator conveniently carried. The artifact itself was even more magnificent than Kovac had anticipated—a falcon crafted from solid gold, its eyes two perfect rubies, its talons clutching a small mechanism that looked incomplete, as if waiting for a missing piece.

Kovac then transferred the falcon to his serving tray, locked the empty case, and departed through a service exit. From acquisition to escape, the operation had taken exactly two minutes and seventeen seconds—a personal best for a high-value theft.

Now, as he lay on the rooftop with the falcon secured in his bag, Kovac focused on his primary objective.

The Guardian Angel herself. She was the main focus.

Kovac shifted his position slightly, ignoring the warm copper beneath him as he adjusted his aim. The experimental rifle hummed in his hands, its advanced targeting systems coming alive with a soft electronic pulse. The scope's display showed Anna's heat signature still crouched behind the walkway's entrance, her form a bright orange glow against the cooler blues of the structure.

He inhaled slowly, counting the seconds between heartbeats. One... two... three... The rhythm of his pulse slowed, a technique he'd mastered through thousands of hours of practice. His breathing became shallow, almost imperceptible, eliminating even the slightest barrel movement that respiration might cause.

The targeting computer flashed green, indicating optimal firing conditions. Wind speed: 3.2 mph from the northwest. Temperature: 89.4 degrees Fahrenheit. Humidity: 27 percent. Distance to target: 327 meters. The scope automatically adjusted for these variables, the crosshairs shifting microscopically to compensate.

Kovac's finger caressed the trigger, applying 2.2 pounds of pressure—just shy of the 2.5 pounds needed for discharge. He waited, patient as death itself. The Guardian Angel would have to move eventually. No prey remained still forever.

Kovac watched through his scope as seconds turned to minutes. The Guardian Angel remained stubbornly in cover, her heat signature pulsing with life behind the metal barrier. Most targets would panic in such a situation—make a desperate dash for safety or call frantically for backup. Not her. She waited, calculating, patient as a predator herself.

He adjusted his position minutely, the copper roofing starting to feel warm against his chest and elbows. Sweat traced a path down his temple, but he ignored it, maintaining focus on his target.

"Come out, come out, wherever you are," Kovac whispered, his lips barely moving. "The dance awaits us, Guardian Angel."

Then—movement. Kovac's finger tensed on the trigger as Anna's heat signature shifted. But instead of emerging from the doorway as expected, she did something bizarre. The thermal imaging showed her body dropping suddenly, disappearing from view.

Kovac frowned, momentarily confused. Had she somehow detected his position? Impossible. His hiding place was perfect, his figure concealed by the carefully arranged ventilation equipment.

His question was answered a moment later when Anna's heat signature reappeared—not at the doorway, but at a maintenance panel in the walkway floor that she had somehow pried open. Kovac's eyes widened in grudging admiration. She was using the service crawlspace beneath the walkway—a route no ordinary person would even know existed, let alone think to use under fire.

"Clever girl," he murmured, tracking her through the thermal scope. The crawlspace ran the length of the walkway, offering her concealed passage—but it would eventually force her to emerge.

Kovac recalculated, anticipating her exit point. The garage end of the walkway had a similar maintenance access panel. He shifted his aim, preparing for her emergence. The targeting computer adjusted to the new coordinates, compensating for the slightly increased distance.

But the Guardian Angel had another surprise in store. Instead of continuing to the end of the crawlspace, her heat signature suddenly veered left, toward a section of the walkway's exterior wall. Kovac watched, puzzled, as she appeared to be working at something—the scan showed her arms moving in short, precise motions.

Then, without warning, a section of the walkway's exterior paneling burst outward, kicked free with explosive force. Before Kovac could adjust his aim, Anna Gabriel launched herself from the opening, her body arcing through the air in a controlled dive.

Kovac fired instinctively, the experimental rifle discharging with nothing more than a soft pneumatic hiss. The bullet cut through the air, its micro-stabilizers adjusting its trajectory—but Anna was moving too fast, her trajectory unpredictable. The shot missed its target by inches, grazing her shoulder rather than finding its mark in her skull.

Anna fell through the air, her body perfectly aligned for the impact to come. The thirty-foot drop would kill most people, or at minimum shatter bones and rupture organs. But Anna wasn't most people. Her eyes locked onto her landing zone—a security guard standing below, his attention on the commotion at the palace's main entrance.

Time seemed to slow as she descended, and Kovac watched, stunned. The guard's black uniform with its silver epaulets. The polished leather of his boots. The radio clipped to his belt, its red light blinking steadily. The way his hand rested casually on his holstered sidearm. The unsuspecting tilt of his head as he spoke into his shoulder mic.

The guard below remained oblivious as death plummeted toward him from above.

Chapter 22

Anna had flung herself thirty feet, and her only chance of avoiding serious injury was to break her fall.

So she'd chosen to hit one of the Albino's retreating guards as he passed by just below the walkway.

The impact came with a sickening thud. The guard crumpled instantly, his body absorbing the worst of the collision. Anna felt something crack beneath her—ribs, maybe his collarbone—as they crashed to the ground together. Pain shot through her left ankle and up her leg, but nothing felt broken. The guard wasn't so lucky. He lay motionless beneath her, his expression shocked, breath knocked from his lungs in a sudden *whoosh*.

Anna rolled clear, ignoring the stabbing pain in her ankle. Adrenaline coursed through her system, dulling the worst of it as she scrambled for cover behind a nearby concrete planter.

The massive pot held an ornamental palm, its fronds providing additional concealment as she pressed her back against its base.

Another gunshot from a roof near the security station fired. It had taken her two shots to locate the assailant.

The bullet struck a second guard directly between the shoulder blades. Its specialized payload activated on impact, the round expanding and fragmenting inside his body cavity. The guard's chest erupted in a spray of crimson as the bullet exited through his sternum, shredding his heart and lungs in its passage. He was dead before his body hit the ground, collapsing in a heap just feet from where Anna crouched.

Blood spattered across the decorative stones of the courtyard, droplets landing on Anna's cheek like warm rain. The dead guard's eyes stared sightlessly at the sky, his expression vacant.

"Casper!" she shouted, her voice carrying across the courtyard. "Shooter on the copper roof! East wing, near the ventilation hub!" She pointed toward a section of roofline where sunlight glinted off something metallic—the barrel of a high-tech rifle partially concealed behind an air-conditioning unit. She hoped Casper or Waldo would be watching her on the aerial drone. The building's copper dome provided the shooter with both elevation and cover, its weathered green patina blending with the foliage of nearby trees.

The palace grounds erupted into chaos. Guards shouted orders in Turkmen and Russian, their boots pounding against stone as they scrambled for defensive positions. Guests in formal attire scattered like startled birds, women in silk gowns and men in tailored suits diving behind marble columns and decorative fountains. Water from an ornamental pool splashed onto the pavement as someone fell into its shallow depths, the surface rippling and distorting the mosaic of exotic fish laid into its floor.

Anna pressed her finger to her earpiece, wincing as feedback screeched through the tiny speaker. "Waldo! Get Beth out now! Use the service tunnel behind the kitchens! Move!" The device crackled with static—the shooter must be using some kind of signal jammer. Through the interference, she could barely make out Waldo's panicked confirmation.

Another shot rang out, the bullet striking the planter inches from Anna's head. Fragments of concrete exploded outward, showering her with dust and debris. A piece grazed her cheek, leaving a thin line of blood that dripped onto the collar of her blouse, staining the cream-colored silk with a spreading crimson blotch.

Anna cataloged her surroundings, identifying potential cover and exit routes. Ten meters to her left, a maintenance door led into the palace's west wing. Twenty meters ahead, the garage structure offered multiple hiding places among the diplomatic vehicles. Between her and either sanctuary lay thirty feet of exposed courtyard, the embellished stone patterns offering no protection from the sniper's aim.

The Albino's convoy was still visible at the far end of the courtyard, four black SUVs with tinted windows forming a protective diamond formation. Their engines rumbled with impatient energy, exhaust fumes creating shimmering heat mirages above their tailpipes. The lead vehicle's door hung open, a security team member frantically gesturing for the others to hurry.

Anna made her decision. She couldn't let the Albino escape—not when they were this close. Not when Beth's family's lives hung in the balance. The pain in her ankle faded to a dull throb as she focused on the immediate threat. The sniper had her pinned down, but she'd faced worse odds. Much worse.

"Casper, I need a distraction," she muttered into her comm, hoping the signal would get through. "Anything. Now."

Before her partner could respond, a new commotion erupted from the palace's main entrance. Prince Abarim stormed into the courtyard, his face contorted with fury. His silk robe billowed around him as he marched forward, surrounded by a phalanx of elite palace guards. Their plain uniforms contrasted the prince's vibrant attire, creating a dark cloud around him.

"There!" the prince shouted, jabbing a bejeweled finger in Anna's direction. "Apprehend her immediately! She is responsible for this chaos! For the theft! For everything!"

The prince's carefully styled hair had come loose in the commotion, strands falling across his forehead in a way that somehow made him look more dangerous than disheveled. The gaudy rings on his fingers caught the sunlight as he gesticulated wildly.

"I want her alive!" he continued, his voice rising to a near scream. "Bring her to me! She will pay for her insolence!"

The palace guards spread out to flank Anna's position. Their weapons—automatic rifles with tactical scopes—were raised and ready. The lead guard barked orders in Turkmen, directing his men to establish a perimeter. Their boots crunched on the pathway, the sound like bones breaking underfoot.

Anna cursed under her breath. The sniper above, the prince's guards closing in, and the Albino's convoy preparing to depart—the situation was deteriorating by the second. She needed to move, and fast, but every direction offered its own deadly threat.

A guard approached her position from the right, his rifle trained on the planter. Anna could see the tension in his trigger finger, the tremor in his hands betraying his nervousness despite his professional demeanor. The sunlight gleamed off his helmet's polished visor.

"Halt!" he commanded in heavily accented English. "Hands where I can see them!"

Anna remained motionless. The guard took another step forward, his boot crushing a fallen jasmine blossom, releasing its sweet fragrance into the air.

"I will not repeat myself," the guard warned, his voice hardening. "Show yourself now, or we will open fire!"

Anna remained where she was, listening. She peered through a gap in the fractured planter.

Through the gap, she counted the security detail surrounding Prince Abarim. One. Two. Three. Ten in total. Ten highly trained men with automatic weapons, body armor, and a thirst for revenge. They bore the insignia of the presidential guard—men selected for their loyalty, their ruthlessness, and their willingness to follow orders without question.

Meanwhile, the Albino's motorcade was pulling away, tires crunching over gravel as the convoy began its exit. Through the tinted windows of the third vehicle, Anna caught a glimpse of pale skin and white hair—their target, slipping away with whatever information he had about Beth's family.

The lead SUV's engine roared as it accelerated toward the palace gates, followed closely by the others in tight formation. Diplomatic flags fluttered from their hoods, granting them immunity and unquestioned passage through checkpoints. The sound of their powerful engines echoed off the palace walls, a mechanical growl.

"Damn it," she muttered.

In that moment, a decision crystallized in her mind. Her only choice was to move forward, to attack when they expected retreat.

"Casper," she said into her comm, "I'm going to create an opening. Be ready."

Without waiting for a response, Anna burst from behind the planter. She moved with explosive speed, her body a blur as she charged directly toward the prince and his security detail. The guard nearest to her froze in momentary shock—he'd expected her to flee, not attack. That hesitation cost him his life.

Anna's first shot took him cleanly through the forehead, the 9mm round creating a small, neat hole just above his right eyebrow. His body crumpled, knees buckling before he collapsed onto the pavement. His helmet rolled away, coming to rest against the base of the fountain.

The courtyard erupted in gunfire once more. Anna slid behind a marble bench as bullets chipped away at the stone, sending white fragments flying like shrapnel. The bench's legs, carved to resemble lion's paws, offered minimal protection for her crouched form.

"Get down!" Anna shouted to a group of civilians frozen in terror nearby. A woman in an evening gown stood paralyzed, her hands clutching a pearl necklace as if it might somehow protect her. A diplomatic attaché had dropped his briefcase, papers spilling across the ground like oversized confetti. Anna lunged, tackling them both moments before bullets tore through the space they'd occupied.

Prince Abarim was screaming orders blindly. His security detail reformed a protective circle around him, their weapons pointed outward.

Anna glanced upward, trying to locate the sniper on the roof. The copper dome gleamed in the afternoon sun, temporarily blinding her. She blinked away the afterimage, scanning the roofline for any sign of him. Nothing. Had he relocated, or was he simply waiting for a clear shot?

Her earpiece crackled to life. "Anna, it's Beth. We're in the tunnels. Waldo says there's an exit near the eastern perimeter. Are you okay? We heard gunfire."

"Stay in the tunnels," Anna replied tersely, ducking as another burst of gunfire shattered an urn near her position. "Don't emerge until Casper gives the all clear."

The Albino's convoy had reached the palace gates, the lead SUV already passing through. In moments, they would be gone, taking with them any hope of finding Beth's family.

No more distractions. She needed to keep moving.

She attacked again. Two more shots. Two more men down.

She went for cover. A bullet sliced across her arm. A flash from the sniper's perch.

She dove.

Another bullet punched a soccer ball–sized hole in the flagstones where she'd been standing moments before. At least the sniper had distracted the prince's men.

Anna fired three more shots.

Six of the guards were now dead on the ground. She took cover again. More bullets struck the bench. Flecks of stone peppered her face. She winced against the deluge. Memories of hot sand and shouting voices echoed in her mind.

Four guards and the prince remained, their formation breaking down as panic set in. The bodies of their fallen comrades lay scattered across the courtyard like discarded chess pieces.

It was time to cut off the head of the snake.

Anna moved with lethal fluidity, her body operating on muscle memory honed through thousands of hours of SEAL training. She executed a combat roll across the exposed courtyard, each movement calculated to minimize her profile. The roll distributed impact forces across her shoulder blades, protected her weapon, and kept her center of mass low—a technique perfected in the kill houses of Coronado.

As she came up from the roll, Anna transitioned seamlessly into a modified Center Axis Relock stance—a shooting position developed for extreme close-quarters combat. Her elbows tucked tight against her torso, weapon centered at sternum level, shoulders squared to the target. This positioning maximized accuracy while minimizing exposure, creating the smallest possible target for the remaining guards.

The first remaining guard barely had time to register her movement before Anna squeezed the trigger twice in rapid succession. She employed the SEAL-taught "controlled pair" technique—two shots delivered in precise rhythm, the second round fired exactly as the weapon settled from the first shot's recoil. Both bullets struck the guard's throat just above his body armor, severing his carotid artery and trachea simultaneously. He dropped his weapon, hands clutching futilely at his neck as arterial blood sprayed in a pulsing arc across the stones.

Anna was already moving to her next target, executing what instructors called the "flow state"—a condition where conscious thought gave way to pure tactical response. Her eyes registered threats, her body responded, all without the delay of deliberate consideration. Each movement turned into the next with machine-like efficiency.

She fired a single round into the decorative fountain's pump housing. Water erupted in a pressurized geyser, temporarily obscuring the remaining guard's vision. In that split-second of blindness, Anna closed the distance. Her hand shot out in a modified knife-hand strike, the hardened edge of her palm crushing the guard's larynx with concentrated force. As he staggered backward, Anna's follow-up strike drove his nasal cartilage into his brain. He was dead before his back hit the ground, his unseeing eyes reflecting the azure Turkmen sky.

The remaining two guards positioned themselves between Anna and the prince, their weapons raised in tactical shooting stances.

She fired between them, splitting bowling pins.

The prince's snarl died at the same time he did.

He toppled backwards, and his remaining guards screamed and fled.

By this time, Anna was sprinting toward the guard complex. The sniper's rifle could still be seen on the roof.

What range would that sniper have? The weapon seemed to possess special tactical advantages. Too accurate to be a normal rifle.

No time to think. The sniper first.

More guards were shouting behind her. More men with automatic weapons were arriving.

Anna's boots pounded along the path. Each step sent jolts of pain through her injured ankle, but she pushed through it, compartmentalizing the sensation as she'd been trained.

The complex loomed ahead—a three-story structure of weathered stone and reinforced concrete attached to the palace's eastern wing. Narrow windows like gun slits punctuated the facade, designed more for defense than aesthetics.

Anna spotted a maintenance ladder bolted to the building's rear wall—a simple metal construction, its rungs worn smooth from years of use. Rust had formed at the joints where the ladder met the stone, creating reddish-brown stains that trailed down the wall like dried blood. The ladder extended upward, disappearing over the edge of the copper roofline.

Without hesitation, she grabbed the first rung and began to climb.

Chapter 23

The metal was hot to the touch, baked by hours of direct sunlight. Her injured ankle protested with each upward movement, but she maintained a steady pace, her breathing even. The sounds of chaos from the courtyard grew more distant—shouts in Turkmen, the wail of approaching sirens, the crackle of radio communications as security forces attempted to restore order.

As she neared the top, Anna slowed her ascent. The final few rungs required her to expose herself momentarily before reaching the roof's surface. If the sniper was watching the ladder, she'd be an easy target—silhouetted against the sky, movement restricted, nowhere to dodge.

Anna paused, listening intently. The copper roof above her creaked slightly as someone moved across its surface—deliberate footsteps, carefully placed. The sniper was still there, perhaps preparing to relocate or setting up for another shot.

Anna pulled a small mirror from her pocket—a simple tactical tool that had saved her life more than once. Carefully angling it above the roofline, she caught a glimpse of the situation.

The roof stretched out in a broad expanse of weathered copper, broken by ventilation ducts, satellite dishes, and ancient chimneys no longer in use. Near the center, partially concealed behind an air-conditioning unit, she spotted the sniper. His back was to her, attention focused on packing his rifle into a specialized case. The weapon itself lay on a portable shooting mat—a sleek, deadly piece of technology unlike any she'd seen before.

Anna holstered her pistol and continued her climb, moving with catlike silence. As her head cleared the roofline, the full panorama of the palace grounds spread out before her. From this elevation, she could see the last of the Albino's motorcade exiting through the main gates, the four black SUVs reaching the boulevard beyond. The Albino was escaping—but she couldn't pursue him yet. First, she had to deal with the immediate threat.

Anna pulled herself onto the roof, her boots making contact with only the faintest whisper of sound. She moved in a low crouch, using the ventilation equipment as cover. The sniper—a tall, lean man—continued methodically packing his equipment, unaware of her approach.

As she drew closer, Anna could make out more details, and her heart hammered as she recognized the man.

Kovac.

His hair was cropped close to his skull in a military cut. His face was streaked with paint. He wore a black tactical suit of unfamiliar design, the material seeming to absorb rather than reflect light. Beside him lay a silver case—not for his weapon, but for something else. Something that gleamed gold within its confines.

The Golden Falcon.

Anna froze, momentarily shocked. So this was why the artifact had vanished from the exhibition—this sniper had somehow stolen it right under everyone's noses.

Her momentary hesitation cost her. Kovac's head tilted slightly, as if sensing a disturbance in the air around him. Without warning, he spun, drawing a combat knife from his belt. The blade—at least nine inches—sliced through the space where Anna's throat had been a split second earlier.

She jerked backward, narrowly avoiding the strike, and launched herself at him. Her first punch connected solidly with his solar plexus, driving the air from his lungs. Most men would have doubled over, giving her time to follow up with a disabling blow. But this man merely grunted, absorbing the impact as if it were nothing more than a minor inconvenience.

His counterattack came with frightening speed—a reverse elbow strike aimed at her temple. Anna ducked beneath it, feeling the displacement of air as his arm whistled over her head. She responded with a low kick to his knee, intending to dislocate the joint and end the fight quickly.

The sniper pivoted at the last moment, taking the kick on his thigh rather than his knee. His eyes locked with hers for the first time, and Anna felt a chill run through her. They were pale, almost colorless, like ice with the faintest tinge of blue. But it wasn't their color that disturbed her—it was the complete absence of emotion in them. No anger, no fear, no determination. As if she were a problem to be solved rather than an opponent to be defeated.

"Guardian Angel," he said, his voice carrying a slight Eastern European accent. "This will be a beautiful thing."

Anna didn't waste breath responding. She launched into a combination attack—jab, cross, hook—each strike carrying into the next. The Albino's motorcade was a quarter mile away now. Half a mile.

She had no time.

The sniper blocked her first two strikes, but her hook caught him along the jaw, snapping his head sideways. Blood spattered from his split lip onto the copper roofing, leaving dark droplets that glinted in the sunlight. He recovered instantly, countering with a lightning-fast combination of his own.

Anna recognized the fighting style immediately—Systema, the Russian martial art favored by Spetsnaz operatives. Fluid, adaptive, and lethal. His strikes contained no wasted energy, each flowing naturally into the next like water finding its path downhill.

The metal beneath their feet creaked and groaned with each shift in weight. Sweat trickled into her eyes, blurring her vision momentarily. She blinked it away, never taking her gaze from her opponent.

But there was no more time for this.

The motorcade was half a mile away. The longest sniper shot in the world was recorded at two miles. She was an expert with most rifles, but the one he was packing seemed different.

Besides, firing a weapon after vigorous physical exertion was a good way to throw off a shot.

She shoved Kovac back, trying to send him stumbling over the edge of the roof.

Just then, a burst of gunfire shattered tiles nearby. More of the soldiers in the palace had spotted them. Voices shouted, pinpointing their location.

But if Kovac felt fear, he didn't show it. His eyes flashed as he slammed his thumb into Anna's throat, using the distraction to his advantage.

Anna's vision exploded with stars as Kovac's thumb connected with her trachea. The strike compressed her airway, sending a shock of panic through her system. Her lungs burned, desperate for oxygen that couldn't pass through. Training took over as she staggered backward, creating distance to recover.

Bullets continued to pepper the rooftop around them, copper fragments flying. The palace guards below had organized themselves enough to provide suppressing fire, though their aim was hampered by the roof's angle. Each impact sent vibrations through the metal beneath Anna's feet.

Kovac moved with predatory dedication, seemingly unconcerned by the gunfire. A bullet grazed his tactical suit, the material rippling oddly where the round made contact but showing no sign of penetration. Some kind of advanced ballistic fiber, Anna realized—technology she'd never encountered before.

"You're good," Kovac acknowledged, circling her. His pale eyes never left hers, studying, calculating. "Better than your file suggested."

Anna finally managed to draw a ragged breath, her throat screaming in protest. "You... have a file on me?" she rasped, buying seconds to recover.

"Of course." Kovac's lips curled into what might have been a smile on anyone else's face. "You've been my study for months. My masterpiece."

A bullet struck between them, throwing up a spray of particles that obscured Kovac's face. Anna used the moment to lunge toward the silver case containing the Golden Falcon. Her fingers had just brushed its surface when Kovac's boot crashed down on her wrist, pinning her hand to the roof.

Pain lanced up her arm as the bones in her wrist compressed under his weight. Anna rolled with the pressure, using her body's momentum to sweep Kovac's supporting leg. As he momentarily lost balance, she wrenched her hand free and scrambled toward the case.

The silver container lay open, the Golden Falcon gleaming within its protective foam housing. The artifact was smaller than Anna had remembered—perhaps ten inches tall—but exquisitely crafted.

Kovac recovered quickly, launching himself at Anna. His knife slashed downward in a killing arc, aimed at the junction of her neck and shoulder. Anna twisted away, feeling the blade slice through her jacket and bite into the flesh of her upper arm. Hot blood welled from the wound, soaking into the torn fabric.

More gunfire erupted from below. The guards had adjusted their position, their aim improving. Bullets ricocheted off ventilation ducts and punched through the weaker sections of roofing. One round struck the silver case, sending it skidding across the copper surface toward the edge.

Anna lunged for it, her fingers closing around the handle just as it teetered on the brink. The movement put her directly in Kovac's path, and he didn't hesitate. His knife slashed downward again, this time catching her across the back. Fire spread along her spine as the blade cut through jacket, shirt, and skin in one clean stroke.

Anna bit back a scream, channeling the pain into desperate strength. She twisted away from the edge, the silver case clutched against her chest like a shield. Blood ran down her back in warm rivulets, soaking into her waistband. Each movement sent fresh waves of agony through her nervous system, but she forced herself to get through it.

Kovac advanced, his knife held in a reverse grip that maximized its cutting potential. His skin was spattered with blood—some his, most hers. The gunfire intensified around them, bullets creating a deadly hailstorm.

Anna's fingers closed around the Golden Falcon, feeling its surprising weight and solidity. The gold was cold against her skin despite the afternoon heat. The artifact's edges were sharp, its wings extended in an aerodynamic curve that fit perfectly in her grasp.

Kovac lunged again, his knife aimed directly at her throat. Anna pivoted, bringing the Golden Falcon up in a desperate arc. The solid gold connected with Kovac's wrist with a sickening crack. Bones shattered under the impact, and the knife clattered to the copper roofing, spinning away toward a ventilation duct.

Kovac didn't cry out, didn't even flinch. He simply adjusted, his uninjured hand shooting out to grab Anna's throat. His fingers found her previous injury, pressing into the already damaged tissue. Black spots danced at the edges of her vision.

She struck him again. And again.

The Golden Falcon's beak connected with Kovac's temple with savage force. The impact resonated through the ancient artifact, up Anna's arm, and into her shoulder. Blood erupted from the wound, spattering across the weathered roof.

For the first time, emotion flickered across Kovac's face—not pain, but something almost like surprise. His grip on her throat loosened fractionally, and Anna seized the opportunity. She drove her knee upward into his solar plexus, simultaneously twisting free of his grasp. Air rushed back into her lungs, sweet and painful.

Kovac staggered backward, one hand pressed to his temple where blood poured between his fingers. The wound was deep—bone visible beneath torn flesh—yet he remained standing, his pale eyes fixed on Anna with undiminished intensity.

Before Anna could respond, Kovac did something unexpected. He smiled—a genuine expression that transformed his face to something almost human. Then he stepped backward off the roof, his body dropping from sight.

Anna rushed to the edge, the Golden Falcon still clutched in her bloodied hand. Looking down, she expected to see Kovac's broken body on the courtyard pavement. Instead, she glimpsed a black tactical rope whipping in the wind, secured to a pipe. In the distance, a figure in black sprinted across the palace grounds, moving with impossible speed for someone with his injuries.

"Casper!" Anna shouted into her comm. "Target heading east! Intercept if possible!"

Only static answered her call. The system was still being jammed.

Pain washed over her in waves as her adrenaline began to ebb. The knife wound across her back burned like a line of fire, and her damaged throat made each breath an exercise in agony. Blood loss was becoming a concern—her clothing was soaked with it, leaving crimson footprints on the roof wherever she moved.

But she still had a shot to make.

This was the reason she'd ascended to the roof.

Anna staggered toward the abandoned rifle. The weapon lay where Kovac had left it. Unlike any rifle she'd ever handled, its sleek design spoke of cutting-edge technology and unlimited resources.

She dropped to one knee beside it, wincing as the movement pulled at the wound across her back. The Golden Falcon sat heavily on her lap as she examined the rifle. Its scope was unlike anything she'd seen before—a digital interface with thermal overlay capabilities and what appeared to be a targeting computer built into the housing.

Anna peered through the scope, surprised at the clarity of the image. The Albino's convoy was nearly a mile away, the four black SUVs moving in tight formation down the boulevard. The scope automatically adjusted, compensating for distance, wind, and bullet drop. A small joystick near the trigger guard caught her attention—some kind of manual targeting system.

Her finger found the trigger, testing its resistance. Approximately 2.5 pounds of pressure would send the round downrange. She centered the crosshairs on the lead vehicle, then reconsidered. The principal would be in the third SUV—standard security protocol for high-value targets.

The scope's digital readout provided real-time data: distance to target 1.47 miles, wind speed 4.3 mph from the northwest, ambient temperature 91.2 degrees Fahrenheit. The targeting computer calculated bullet drop and suggested minute adjustments to her aim.

Anna inhaled deeply, ignoring the pain from her various wounds. She held the breath at the top, feeling her heartbeat slow as she entered the shooter's mindset. Time seemed to stretch, the world narrowing to the view through the scope.

She squeezed the trigger.

Chapter 24

Anna was breathing heavily, using an unfamiliar weapon at an impossible range...

The odds weren't in her favor as she fired.

The rifle discharged with a soft hiss rather than the expected crack. The round left the barrel at hypersonic speed, its trajectory a perfect arc toward the distant target. Through the scope, Anna watched as the bullet closed the distance in less than two seconds.

The round struck the third SUV's tire, the specially designed ammunition detonating on impact. The vehicle swerved violently, then flipped, rolling across the boulevard in a shower of glass and metal. The remaining vehicles in the convoy scattered, security personnel pouring out with weapons drawn.

Anna adjusted her aim, focusing on the chaos below. Through the scope, she spotted a pale figure emerging from the overturned SUV. The Albino appeared uninjured, moving with the same efficiency she'd witnessed at the exhibition. He carried a case identical to the one that had contained the Golden Falcon.

She centered the crosshairs on his chest, finger tensing on the trigger. One more shot and it would be over.

But they needed the Albino alive. She had to keep him from reaching one of the other vehicles.

"Casper!" she barked into her comms.

A pause. Then a crackle and a voice replied. "I'm here! We're back up!"

"I need you to ascertain a package," she insisted.

A pause. "What... sort of package?"

More bullets struck the roof. Anna could hear voices beneath her. Voices on the ladder behind her.

Not much time.

"That package at mile marker 5.2, boulevard east," Anna said quickly. "The pale one. Alive, not dead. I need intel." She adjusted her aim as more bullets sparked around her. "Get a vehicle. Get there now. I'll find my own way out."

"Anna, you're injured. I can hear it in your voice," Casper replied, concern evident despite the comm interference.

"Now, Casper!" Anna insisted, the effort sending fresh pain through her damaged throat. "Before he slips away again."

She watched through the scope as the Albino conferred with his security team. No panic despite the precariousness of his situation. His white hair stood out starkly against the dark tactical gear of his men.

"Copy that," Casper finally responded. "Moving to intercept. Waldo's tracking Beth's signal. They're clear of the palace, headed to the extraction point."

Anna allowed herself a moment of relief before refocusing on the task at hand. The guards were getting closer. She could hear boots on the ladder rungs, the metal groaning under their weight. Maybe thirty seconds before they reached the roof.

Through the scope, Anna watched as one of the Albino's men approached with a satellite phone. The guard's uniform was immaculate despite the crash—gear with no identifying insignia, boots polished to a mirror shine. His movements were professional as he handed the device to his employer.

Anna adjusted her aim and squeezed the trigger. The round traveled the 1.5 miles in less than two seconds, striking the satellite phone with devastating effect. The device exploded in a shower of plastic and circuitry, taking three of the guard's fingers with it. Blood spattered across the Albino's pale face as his subordinate collapsed, clutching his mutilated hand.

The message was clear: no communications, no escape, no help.

The Albino's head snapped up, his eyes scanning the distant rooftops. Even at this range, Anna could see the cunning in his expression. He knew exactly where the shot had come from. Their eyes seemed to meet across the impossible distance, a moment of recognition.

Another guard rushed forward, attempting to usher the Albino toward the nearest intact SUV. The vehicle's engine was already running, exhaust fumes circling above its dual tailpipes. Its reinforced door stood open, offering armored sanctuary.

Anna's finger found the trigger again. The rifle whispered its deadly song. The guard's head snapped backward as the round found its mark, his body collapsing in a heap of pooling blood. His sidearm—an SIG Sauer with custom grip—clattered across the pavement, coming to rest against the curb where water from a recent rainfall still collected in shallow pools.

The Albino flung himself behind the open SUV door, using its armored bulk as a shield against further shots. His movements betrayed years of combat experience. Through the scope, Anna watched as he signaled his remaining men, gesturing in sharp motions that conveyed clear instructions despite the distance.

Anna fired again, the bullet punching through the SUV's front tire. The vehicle listed to one side as air hissed from the punctured rubber. Another shot disabled the engine block, sending steam billowing from beneath the hood like a wounded animal's dying breath. Oil and coolant leaked onto the pavement, forming rainbow-slicked puddles.

The footsteps on the ladder grew louder. Anna had seconds, not minutes.

She lined up one more shot, aiming for the Albino's silver case. If it contained what she suspected—the Silver Falcon that complemented her Golden one—destroying it might force his hand. The scope's targeting computer calculated the adjustments, compensating for the case's partial concealment behind the vehicle door.

Anna squeezed the trigger a final time.

The round struck the case's edge, blowing the locking mechanism apart in a shower of metal fragments. The case flew from the Albino's grasp, its contents spilling across the boulevard.

And there it was—the Silver Falcon, nearly identical to its golden counterpart except for its metallic hue. It skittered across the pavement, coming to rest in full view.

The first guard's head appeared above the roofline, his weapon already raised. Anna abandoned the rifle, snatching up the Golden Falcon and rolling away as bullets tore into the copper where she'd been kneeling. Blood loss and exhaustion slowed her movements, but desperation lent her strength.

She needed an exit strategy. The ladder was compromised. The edges of the roof presented a three-story drop to unyielding stone—possibly survivable with proper technique, but not in her current condition. Her gaze fell on Kovac's abandoned rope, still secured to the pipe.

Anna staggered toward it, clutching the Golden Falcon against her chest. The artifact seemed to pulse with ancient energy, its weight both burden and comfort. Through the scope, she'd seen its silver counterpart—the two pieces designed to fit together, forming a key to something of immense value. Something worth killing for.

More guards emerged onto the rooftop, their weapons tracking her movement. Anna reached the rope, looping it around her forearm as bullets followed her. The Golden Falcon's sharp wing sliced into her palm as she gripped it tighter, blood making the ancient gold slick against her skin.

With no time for proper rappelling technique, Anna simply jumped, letting gravity and the rope's friction control her descent. The rough material burned through her jacket sleeve and into the flesh beneath, adding fresh pain to her catalog of injuries. The wound across her back screamed in protest.

Blood—both dried and fresh—made her grip treacherous, the rope slipping through her fingers faster than she intended.

Twenty feet from the ground, the rope suddenly went slack. Above, a guard had cut it with a combat knife, his face filled with vindictive satisfaction as the severed end whipped past Anna's cheek.

She tucked and rolled as she hit the ground, distributing the impact across her shoulder and hip. The technique saved her from broken bones but couldn't prevent the jarring collision that knocked the breath from her lungs. The Golden Falcon dug into her ribs, its sharp wings leaving fresh cuts across her torso.

Anna lay stunned for precious seconds, her vision swimming with black spots. Shouts echoed around her as palace guards converged on her position. The courtyard stones felt cool against her cheek, a small mercy amid overwhelming pain.

But there was no time to wait. No time to just lie there.

She had to *move*.

"Casper," she whispered into her comm. "Status?"

Static hissed in her ear for a moment before Casper's voice came through, strained but clear. "Moving to intercept target. Waldo has a vehicle. Three minutes to your position."

"Too long," Anna murmured. The guards were closing in, their weapons steady in practiced hands.

Despite her injuries, Anna rolled onto her back and broke into a dead sprint. The stretch limousine their billionaire companion had used still rested where it had been parked in the motor lot.

She'd spotted a chauffeur abandon the vehicle when the shooting had started.

Had he left the keys?

Who grabs keys when running for their life?

A crap shoot. A limousine wasn't exactly a great getaway vehicle, but she was in no state to be picky.

Bullets ricocheted off the ground at her feet as she zig-zagged, trying to place cover between her and the majority of the security forces.

Military men were appearing at the gate, pointing automatic weapons at her.

The limousine's driver-side door was unlocked. Anna yanked it open and fell into the seat, leaving a smear of blood across the pristine leather. Her trembling fingers searched the ignition—no keys. Of course not. That would've been too easy.

"Come on," she hissed, reaching under the steering column. With practiced movements, she tore away the plastic housing, exposing the wiring beneath. The Golden Falcon sat heavily in her lap, its ruby eyes seeming to watch her as she worked.

Bullets struck the limousine's body with metallic pings, some penetrating the thin door panels. The windshield spider-webbed as a round struck it but didn't break—bulletproof glass, at least. Small mercies.

Anna stripped two wires with her teeth, wincing as the copper taste mixed with blood in her mouth. She twisted them together, and the limousine's dashboard lit up. The engine coughed once, then roared to life.

"Yes," she whispered, shifting into drive. The vehicle lurched forward as she pressed the accelerator, its long body unwieldy compared to the tactical vehicles she was accustomed to driving. The limousine's bulk worked in her favor now, though, as bullets that would have shredded a smaller car merely dented its reinforced panels.

Anna aimed the limousine directly at the palace gates, where military personnel had established a hasty blockade. Their faces registered shock as twelve feet of armored luxury vehicle barreled toward them at increasing speed. Most scattered, diving for cover as the limousine crashed through the makeshift barrier.

The impact jolted Anna forward, reopening the wound across her back. Fresh blood soaked into the driver's seat as she fought to maintain control of the vehicle. The Golden Falcon slid from her lap onto the floor, its weight making a dull thud against the carpet.

Once through the gates, Anna swerved onto the boulevard, tires screaming in protest at the sharp turn. The limousine's rear end fishtailed, taking out a lamppost before she regained control. In the rearview mirror, she could see palace security scrambling for vehicles to pursue her.

"Casper," she gasped into her comm, "heading east on the main boulevard. Where's the Albino?"

"Still at the crash site," Casper replied, his voice tight. "Military's converging. It's turning into a standoff."

Anna calculated quickly. The Albino was approximately a mile ahead. If she could reach him before the military surrounded the area completely...

She pressed the accelerator to the floor, feeling the limousine surge forward with surprising power for its size. The engine's roar filled the cabin as the speedometer climbed past eighty, then ninety. Blood loss made her lightheaded, her vision occasionally blurring around the edges. She blinked hard, forcing herself to focus on the road ahead.

Chapter 25

She gripped the steering wheel tighter, the pain in her lacerated palm providing the shock of clarity she needed.

Through the windshield, she could make out the overturned SUV, its black bulk resting on its side like a wounded beast. Military vehicles had formed a perimeter around the crash site, uniformed personnel crouching behind open doors with weapons raised. The Albino stood in the center, his white hair visible even at this distance.

Anna pressed the accelerator harder, pushing the limousine to its limits. The vehicle wasn't built for speed, but its weight and momentum would serve her purpose. She needed to break through that perimeter, to reach the Albino before he disappeared again—taking with him any hope of finding Beth's family.

Her earpiece crackled. "Anna, what are you doing?" Casper's voice was sharp with concern. "The military has the area locked down. You'll never get through."

"Watch me," Anna muttered, her eyes fixed on the approaching scene.

The first military checkpoint loomed ahead—a hastily established barricade of vehicles and armed personnel. They'd spotted the approaching limousine, weapons swinging in her direction. Warning shots kicked up asphalt near the vehicle's front tires.

Anna didn't slow down. Instead, she aimed the limousine's bulk directly at the weakest point in their formation—the gap between two troop carriers where soldiers were still deploying. The limousine's reinforced front end smashed through, sending men scrambling for safety as the vehicle bulldozed past their position.

She was close enough to see the Albino clearly. He clutched the Silver Falcon in one hand. His face betrayed no emotion as he watched the limousine approach—only cold calculation, as if running tactical scenarios in his head.

The military was closing in from all sides, their discipline evident in their coordinated movements. Turkmen special forces in desert camouflage. They were seconds away from taking the Albino into custody.

Anna couldn't let that happen. If he disappeared into a military detention facility, they might never extract the information they needed.

With a final surge of desperate strength, Anna aimed the limousine directly at the knot of men surrounding the Albino. The vehicle crashed through the final perimeter, sending soldiers diving for cover. The Albino stood his ground until the last possible moment before launching himself sideways as the limousine slammed into the overturned SUV. The impact sent Anna lurching forward, her forehead striking the steering wheel despite the airbag's deployment. Blood cascaded down her face, mingling with sweat and grime.

Through the shattered windshield, Anna saw the Albino sprawled on the pavement twenty feet away. The Silver Falcon had skittered from his grasp, coming to rest near the limousine's crumpled front end. Military personnel were regrouping, weapons trained on both Anna and the Albino.

Anna forced the driver's door open, her body protesting every movement. She stumbled out, one hand clutching the Golden Falcon, the other braced against the limousine's hood for support. Blood dripped steadily from her numerous wounds, creating a trail behind her as she staggered toward the Albino.

He was already rising, his movements intentional despite the situation. His pale eyes locked with hers across the debris-strewn boulevard. For a moment, neither moved.

And then she realized her horrible mistake.

This wasn't the same man.

He was close. Someone had gone to great lengths to make the body double *appear* like the Albino.

But this man wasn't the one she'd encountered back in their small, idyllic hometown. This wasn't the man who'd taken Beth's family.

He was a decoy.

A double.

They'd been tricked.

The man smiled at her, his teeth bloody, his pink eyes glaring. "Too late," he hissed. "Far, far too late. He's gone. Been gone for days, Anna Gabriel.".

Anna had no time to process the information. He was their only source of intel. They needed him alive.

Military men were closing in. Gunshots echoed. She snatched the decoy by the arm, dragging him back to the limousine.

"Casper!" she shouted into her comms. "Where are you?"

But just then, there was a loud shot. A man aiming his pistol at her went down. Two more men by the SUV were struck by distant sniper fire.

Casper. The ghost was providing overwatch.

Her earpiece buzzed.

"Northwest corner, blue sedan," Casper's voice came through, calm and reassuring. "Forty meters and closing."

Anna dragged the Albino decoy by the arm, her grip vise-like despite her injuries. His resistance was token at best—his bloody smile suggesting that he found their situation amusing rather than dire.

"You're bleeding out, Guardian Angel," he taunted, eyes gleaming with malicious delight.

Another shot from Casper's position dropped a soldier who'd been lining up a kill shot. The military forces were regrouping, and shouted orders carried across the debris-strewn boulevard as commanders attempted to restore order.

Anna spotted Casper's blue sedan weaving through the scene, its tires squealing as it navigated around abandoned vehicles and scattered personnel. The car skidded to a stop twenty feet away, its passenger door flying open.

Waldo was driving. Beth was in the back, clutching her emergency oversize bag to her chest.

Casper leaned out the passenger window, rifle in hand.

"Move!" Casper shouted, providing covering fire.

Anna shoved the decoy forward, one hand still clutching the Golden Falcon. Blood loss and exhaustion made each step an effort, her vision narrowing to a tunnel focused solely on the waiting vehicle.

The decoy stumbled, nearly falling. Anna yanked him upright, her fingers digging into his arm with surprising strength. "Move or die," she warned, her voice barely audible over the gunfire.

Something in her tone must have convinced him. The decoy straightened, his movements becoming more cooperative as they closed the distance to Casper's vehicle. Anna's boot connected with something metallic—the Silver Falcon, lying forgotten amid the debris. She scooped it up without breaking stride, tucking it against her body alongside its golden counterpart.

They reached the sedan just as a new wave of military vehicles swarmed into the area. Casper leaned across, pulling the body double into the back seat as Anna collapsed into the passenger side. The door had barely closed before Waldo accelerated, the sedan's engine grumbling as he pushed it to its limits.

"Beth?" Anna gasped, her breathing labored as blood soaked into the sedan's upholstery.

"I'm here," Beth's voice came from the back seat, shaky but determined. She leaned forward, pressing her hand against the worst of Anna's wounds. "You're bleeding badly."

Anna turned her head, vision swimming as she tried to focus on her sister's face. Beth looked pale, her eyes white with fear, but her hands remained steady as she applied pressure to the gash across Anna's back.

"The falcons," Anna murmured, her grip tightening on the golden artifact. "We have both pieces. Put them in that bag of yours. Remove the trail mix."

Beth nodded, hurriedly accepting both pieces.

Waldo navigated the sedan through side streets, avoiding the main thoroughfares where military checkpoints would be established. The vehicle swerved hard around corners, tires squealing in protest. In the back seat, the Albino decoy sat quietly, his pink eyes watching the proceedings with detached amusement.

"Who are you?" Anna demanded, twisting painfully to face him. "Where is the real Albino?"

The man's bloody smile widened. "I am nobody. A ghost. A shadow." His accent was Eastern European, his English perfect despite it. "And my employer? He is gone."

Waldo glanced in the rearview mirror, his face tight with concentration as he navigated the unfamiliar streets. "We need to get off the grid. The entire Turkmen military will be looking for us after what happened at the palace."

"The safe house in Dashoguz," Casper said, checking his weapon. "It's our only option."

"Too far," Anna countered, her voice weakening. "Border checkpoint... won't make it."

Beth's hands pressed harder against Anna's wounds, blood seeping between her fingers despite her efforts. "She needs medical attention now. Not in four hours."

The sedan swerved around a produce truck, narrowly avoiding a collision. Horns blared behind them as Waldo cut across three lanes of traffic, heading toward the industrial district on the city's outskirts.

Anna's vision was darkening around the edges, consciousness slipping away despite her efforts to remain alert. The Golden and Silver Falcons lay in her lap, their metallic surfaces bright.

The sedan's engine growled as Waldo pushed it through the streets of Ashgabat. Anna slumped against the door, leaving bloody handprints on the window glass. Each breath came shorter than the last, her chest rising and falling in an irregular rhythm.

"Anna, stay with me," Beth pleaded, her voice cracking. She tore strips from her own shirt, pressing them against her sister's wounds. The makeshift bandages soaked through almost immediately, the fabric turning from pale blue to deep crimson.

The Albino decoy watched with interest from his corner of the back seat. His eyes tracked every movement, his smile never wavering. "The Guardian Angel bleeds like any mortal," he observed, his voice carrying a musical quality despite the gravity of his words. "Such disappointment."

Casper whipped around, pressing his rifle against the man's temple. "One more word and I redecorate this car with your brains."

The decoy's smile only widened, but he fell silent.

Waldo took a sharp turn down an alley barely wide enough for the sedan, scraping paint from both sides as they squeezed through. The industrial district loomed ahead—abandoned factories and warehouses creating a maze of concrete and rusted metal.

"There." Casper pointed to a weathered building with faded Cyrillic lettering across its facade. "Old textile factory. Backup location."

Waldo guided the sedan behind the building, out of sight from the main road. The engine died with a shuddering cough as he cut the ignition. For a moment, no one moved. The only sound was Anna's labored breathing and the tick of the cooling engine.

"Get her inside," Casper ordered, his voice terse with controlled urgency. "I'll handle our guest."

Beth helped Anna from the car, supporting her sister's weight as they staggered toward a rusted service entrance. Blood trailed behind them, leaving a damning path across the cracked concrete. Waldo rushed ahead, working on the padlocked door with tools pulled from his pocket.

Inside, the abandoned factory was a cathedral of shadows. Massive looms stood silent, their metal frames eaten by decades of neglect. Dust motes danced in the few beams of sunlight that penetrated the grime-covered windows. The air smelled of rust, mildew, and industrial chemicals.

"Over here," Waldo called, clearing a space on what had once been a foreman's desk. "Put her down."

Beth eased Anna onto the wooden surface, wincing at her sister's involuntary groan of pain. Anna's face was alarmingly pale, her normally vibrant green eyes dull and unfocused. Blood soaked her clothing, pooling on the desk beneath her.

Her gaze flickered. She let out a slow breath. "Waldo, overwatch. The drone," she instructed, seeing to the tactical necessities even as her consciousness fled.

Then, her vision swam a final time.

It all went dark.

Chapter 26

Anna floated in darkness. Time lost all meaning as she drifted in and out of sensations—sharp pain as something probed her wounds, voices arguing in urgent whispers, the burn of antiseptic, the prick of a needle. These moments came and went, illuminating nothing, explaining nothing.

Sometimes she thought she heard Beth crying. Other times, Casper's steady voice giving orders. Once, she was certain she felt Waldo's nervous energy as he paced nearby, muttering probabilities under his breath. But always, the darkness would reclaim her, pulling her back into its numbing embrace.

When Anna finally opened her eyes, the world was wrapped in shadow. Night had fallen, and the abandoned factory's cavernous interior was illuminated only by a single kerosene lantern placed on a crate several feet away. Its flame wavered in unseen drafts, casting elongated shadows that danced across the weathered brick walls and rusted machinery.

She lay on something firm but not uncomfortable—a makeshift bed assembled from seat cushions salvaged from somewhere within the building. Clean sheets, smelling faintly of detergent, were tucked around her. Her body felt simultaneously distant and hyper-present, the dull throb of her injuries muted by what she assumed were powerful painkillers.

Casper sat on an overturned bucket beside her, his weathered face half-hidden in shadow. His rifle rested across his knees, ready but not threatening. His sunglasses were gone, revealing eyes tired from extended vigilance. He didn't speak when he noticed her consciousness returning, simply offered a slight nod of acknowledgment.

Anna tried to take stock of her condition. Bandages were wrapped around her torso, tight enough to support but not constrict. More covered her left arm and right hand. Something cold and medical-smelling had been spread across the laceration on her cheek. Her throat still ached from Kovac's strike, but the crushing pain had subsided to a manageable discomfort.

She attempted to sit up. Pain lanced through her back, sharp enough to cut through whatever painkillers coursed through her system. A small involuntary sound escaped her lips—not quite a groan, but close enough.

Casper's hand appeared instantly, firm against her shoulder. "Easy," he murmured, his voice barely a whisper. "Beth used thirty-seven stitches just on your back. Others here and there where you needed them most, but we had to used duct tape when we ran out of thread. Try not to pop *any* of them. Your body's stable enough that you're making new blood, but unless we get you a transfusion or a lot more rest..." He let the rest of the sentence hang. They both knew she was aware how delicate people could be, even after they woke up from a bad wound. Most people anyway.

Anna settled back, adjusting to the limitations of her injured body. The factory's vast space stretched around them, its high ceilings lost in darkness. Massive industrial fans hung motionless overhead, their blades thick with dust and cobwebs. In the distance, water dripped like a metronome, each drop echoing through the empty building.

They sat in silence for a long moment, the quiet broken only by that distant dripping and the occasional honking of a distant horn.

"How long?" Anna finally asked, her voice a rasp that barely carried past the kerosene lamp.

"Sixteen hours," Casper replied, shifting his weight on the makeshift seat. The metal bucket creaked under him, the sound amplified by the factory's acoustics. "You lost a lot of blood."

Anna's gaze traveled around their sanctuary. In the far corner, Beth lay curled on another improvised bed, her body rising and falling with the deep, even breaths of exhausted sleep. Her face, just visible in the lamplight, was smudged with dirt and what might have been dried tears. Her right hand still clutched a medical kit, fingers relaxed but not releasing their grip. Blood—Anna's blood—had dried under her fingernails and in the creases of her knuckles.

Near the factory's main entrance, Waldo sat slumped against a concrete pillar, his chin resting on his chest. His laptop lay open beside him, its screen dark to preserve battery. Various electronic devices surrounded him—signal jammers, communication equipment, and surveillance monitors, all carefully arranged for optimal function. His fingers still rested on the keyboard, as if he'd fallen asleep mid-keystroke. A half-eaten protein bar lay forgotten by his side, ants already discovering the treat.

"Our guest?" Anna whispered, careful not to wake the others.

Casper's expression hardened, the lines around his mouth deepening. "Secured. Back room. I rigged a pressure plate alarm in case he tries anything." He gestured toward a heavy metal door partially visible behind a row of decommissioned textile machines. Their massive frames lurked in the dim light, shuttle arms frozen in positions they had held for decades.

"Has he talked?"

"Not usefully." Casper ran a hand over his shaved head, his palm grazing the short stubble. "Lots of cryptic bullshit. Philosophical musings about predators and prey. Nothing concrete about the Albino or Beth's family."

Anna's eyes found the Golden and Silver Falcons, now resting side by side on a wooden crate near her makeshift bed. The artifacts gleamed dully in the lantern light, their surfaces cleaned of blood and grime.

"The Albino is gone?" she asked.

Casper nodded grimly. "Waldo tracked a manifest of a ship owned by one of the Albino's shell companies. Left Türkmenbaşy port three days ago. Our pink-eyed friend was just a distraction to keep us occupied while the real target slipped away."

Anna absorbed this information, trying to make sense of it despite the fog of pain and medication. The concrete floor beneath her makeshift bed radiated cold that seeped through the cushions.

"The falcons," she said, her gaze returning to the artifacts. "Has Waldo figured out what they are?"

"Some kind of key, we think." Casper shifted, his knee joint popping in the silence. "They fit together. When combined, they reveal some kind of mechanism. But without the proper context..." He shrugged, the gesture making his tactical vest creak slightly.

Anna tried again to sit up, this time moving with deliberate slowness. Pain flared across her back as the stitches pulled against damaged tissue, but she managed to achieve a semi-upright position. Sweat gathered on her forehead from the effort, trickling down the line of her jaw.

"Help me up," she instructed, extending her less-injured arm toward Casper.

He hesitated, concern evident in the lines around his eyes. "Beth will have my ass if those stitches tear."

"I need to talk to our guest." Anna's voice left no room for argument, despite its weakened state. "Now, while the others are sleeping."

With obvious reluctance, Casper supported her as she rose from the makeshift bed. Her legs shuddered beneath her weight, muscles weak from blood loss and trauma. The factory floor felt uneven under her bare feet, its concrete surface pitted and cracked from decades of industrial use and subsequent abandonment.

They moved slowly across the open space, navigating around rusted machinery and fallen ceiling tiles. Every step sent ripples of pain through Anna's body, but she compartmentalized it, pushing the sensation to a distant corner of her awareness. The skill had served her well in field operations and training—pain was information, nothing more. Useful data to be processed, not a master to be obeyed.

But she only managed a few steps before her vision clouded.

"No," Casper said finally. "No. Not now. You're done. We can talk to him come morning."

Anna cursed, sliding down to sit on the floor until her head stopped spinning.

"He got away," she whispered. She stared through a large window in the ceiling, watching the night sky as if searching for some answer in the infinite black.

She let out a faint groan, closing her eyes, then opening them again.

"Yeah. He got away," Casper confirmed, his tone grim.

"He knew we were coming."

"Three days ago."

"Byers? Your contact?"

Casper sighed. "I... don't know. But we'll get out of here. I promise you. I'm already working on something."

Anna nodded. She trusted Casper. There weren't many she did, but Casper had proven himself more than once.

She found herself studying his strong jaw, his intense gaze. There was something comforting about his eyes without having them hidden behind sunglasses.

The silence between them stretched, filled only by the ambient sounds of the abandoned factory—creaking metal, distant water drips, the occasional scurrying of some small creature in the walls. Anna found herself studying Casper's face, seeing the exhaustion lines around his eyes, the stubble darkening his jaw, the slight tension in his shoulders that never fully released.

"We need to regroup," she finally said, her voice steadier. "Figure out our next move."

Casper agreed. "The Albino's trail is cold, but not frozen. Waldo's been tracking shipping manifests, financial transactions. If there's a digital footprint, he'll find it."

Anna's gaze drifted back to the artifacts. The Golden Falcon caught the lamplight, its ruby eyes seeming to glow with inner fire. The Silver Falcon beside it appeared more subdued, its surface absorbing rather than reflecting the weak illumination.

"Those are the key," she murmured. "They're valuable. Valuable enough for him to risk his entourage. We have leverage now."

Casper followed her gaze. "Waldo thinks they're older than they look. Maybe ancient. The craftsmanship is too precise for primitive tools, yet the design suggests something pre-modern."

Anna felt a chill that had nothing to do with her injuries or the factory air. "Help me back. I need to rest before I fall over."

He supported her return journey to the makeshift bed, his movements gentle. As he helped her settle back onto the cushions, his hand lingered briefly on her shoulder—a touch of reassurance rather than necessity.

"Get some sleep," he advised, adjusting the thin blanket over her. "Dawn's in three hours. We move then."

Anna closed her eyes, her body surrendering to exhaustion despite her mind's resistance. The last thing she registered was Casper resuming his position on the overturned bucket, rifle across his knees, gaze fixed on the factory's main entrance. Watchful. Vigilant. Ready. She noticed something else, though...

A mirroring of that same feeling she'd experienced back on the ship. A sort of loneliness, deep in his gaze.

The darkness welcomed her again, but this time it was the darkness of healing sleep rather than unconsciousness. Her last coherent thought was of Beth's children, their faces clear in her mind despite the years since she'd seen them. Wherever they were, whatever the Albino wanted them for, she would find them. The trail wasn't cold yet. And Anna Gabriel had tracked men across worse terrain than this.

This was her promise to the darkness. Her vow to herself. Her oath to Beth.

And Anna Gabriel had never broken an oath.

What's Next for Anna?

Book 5 - Guardian's Mission

She infiltrated hell with one mission—kill the devil before he slips away.

Ex-Navy SEAL Anna Gabriel has survived war zones, black ops, and betrayal—but nothing prepared her for Russia's most brutal prison. To stop a deadly arms dealer from flooding the world with chaos, Anna gets herself locked behind bars, armed with nothing but her wits and her will to survive. And with this arm's dealer, it's personal.

Inside, the rules are written in blood, and enemies lurk in every shadow. To reach her target, Anna must navigate savage gangs, corrupt guards, and a prison warden who plays a deadlier game than she imagined. Time is running out, and failure isn't just death.

In a place where mercy doesn't exist, Anna Gabriel must become the most dangerous predator of all.

Also by Georgia Wagner

Once a rising star in the FBI, with the best case closure rate of any investigator, Ella Porter is now exiled to a small gold mining town bordering the wilderness of Alaska. The reason for her new assignment? She allowed a prolific serial killer to escape custody.

But what no one knows is that she did it on purpose.

The day she shows up in Nome, bags still unpacked, the wife of the richest gold miner in town goes missing. This is the second woman to vanish in as many days. And it's up to Ella to find out what happened.

Assigning Ella to Nome is no accident, either. Though she swore she'd never return, Ella grew up in the small, gold mining town, treated like royalty as a child due to her own family's wealth. But like all gold tycoons, the Porter family secrets are as dark as Ella's own.

Also by Georgia Wagner

The skeletons in her closet are twitching...

Genius chess master and FBI consultant Artemis Blythe swore she'd never return to the misty Cascade Mountains.

Her father—a notorious serial killer, responsible for the deaths of seven women—is now imprisoned, in no small part due to a clue she provided nearly fifteen years ago.

GUARDIAN FOR HIRE

And now her father wants his vengeance.

A new serial killer is hunting the wealthy and the elite in the town of Pinelake. Artemis' father claims he knows the identity of the killer, but he'll only tell daughter dearest. Against her will, she finds herself forced back to her old stomping grounds.

Once known as a child chess prodigy, now the locals only think of her as 'The Ghostkiller's' daughter.

In the face of a shamed family name and a brother involved with the Seattle mob, Artemis endeavours to use her tactical genius to solve the baffling case. Hunting a murderer who strikes without a trace, if she fails, the next skeleton in her closet will be her own.

Want to know more?

Want to see what else the Greenfield authors have written? Go to the website.

https://greenfieldpress.co.uk/

Or sign up to our newsletter where you will get sneak peeks, exclusive giveaways, behind the scenes content, and more. Plus, you'll be notified of Fan Pricing events when they occur and get exclusive offers from other authors.

https://greenfieldpress.co.uk/newsletter/

Prefer social media? Join our thriving Facebook community.

Want to join the inner circle where you can keep up to date with everything? This is a free page on Facebook where you can hang out with likeminded individuals and enjoy discussing my books.

There is cake too (but only if you bring it).

https://www.facebook.com/GreenfieldPress

About the Author

Georgia Wagner worked as a ghost writer for many, many years before finally taking the plunge into self-publishing. Location and character are two big factors for Georgia, and getting those right allows the story to flow seamlessly onto the page. And flow it does, because Georgia is so prolific a new term is required to describe the rate at which nerve-tingling stories find their way into print.

When not found attached to a laptop, Georgia likes spending time in local arboretums, among the trees and ponds. An avid cultivator of orchids, begonias, and all things floral, Georgia also has a strong penchant for art, paintings, and sculptures.